WARLORDS OF THE WEST:

A STORY OF THE COMANCHE

by
PRESTON HARPER

Illustrated by Jack Maxwell

BORDERLANDS

PRESS

BORDERLANDS PRESS
GULF BREEZE, FLORIDA

———

Published by Borderlands Press, 77 Baybridge Gulf Breeze, Florida
32561. Copyright© 1989 by Preston Harper All rights reserved. No part
of this book may be reproduced or transmitted without the written
permission of the Publisher, except where permitted by law. Borderlands logo is patented.

ISBN - 0-9621792-0-5

Book Design *Mel Ristau/Design*
Printed in the United States of America

———

for
MARSHA

CONTENTS

Introduction by John Robinson
ix

Comanche Country
xi
The House of Long Lance
xii

1.
The War Party
Long Lance, principal war chief of the Antelope band,
leads a war party against the invading Apache.
1

2.
The Vision Quest
Eagle, son of Long Lance, undergoes the Comanche rite
of passage.
21

3.
The White Buffalo
Eagle seeks revenge on a murderous buffalo thought by
the Antelope band to be sacred.
23

4.
The Mustang

Talks to Horses, brother of Eagle, sets out to capture the most beautiful wild mustang anyone has ever seen.

45

5.
The Champion

After the abduction of his wife by Coyote Droppings, Talks to Horses asks Eagle to win her back in mortal combat.

57

6.
The Chase

Moonflower, a lovely young maiden of the Antelope band, is attacked by a vicious grizzly bear.

71

7.
The Courting

Eagle, now a great Antelope war chief, is persuaded by Talks to Horses to seek a wife.

85

8.
The Birth

Moonflower's life hangs in the balance as she tries to give birth to a child.

101

9.
The Vengeance Raid

Broken Foot asks Eagle to lead a vengeance raid against the Utes that killed his last son.

115

10.
The Captive: Juan

Eagle and his blood brother, Juan Horse, raid an hacienda in Mexico in an attempt to avenge the death of Juan's father.

131

11.
The Captive: Teresa

Juan's sister and her baby Ana are captured by the sadistic Kicking Bird, a chief of the Penateka band.

143

12.
The Ambush
Iron Bow and Hunting Horse, Eagle's sons, make the
mistake of attacking a long-knife wagon.
157

13.
The Small Warrior
Iron Bow attempts to save the soul of his son Fighting
Heart, who has a terminal illness.
173

14.
The Grand Coup
Iron Bow undertakes single-handedly to save the Antelope band from a troop of long-knife cavalry.
185

Selected Bibliography
203

INTRODUCTION

Comanche! The dread name drove fear through the hearts of westering Americans. But these restless marauders also stirred reluctant respect for their unparalleled horsemanship, even from those who feared them most. Without peer as riders, for two hundred years these terrors of the southwestern plains ranged unchecked from Colorado to Texas, even raiding deeply into Mexico. Yet few of their victims knew anything of their life beyond a terrifying yell or a sudden lance; it is this fuller story that Preston Harper tells so excitingly in the following chapters.

Leaving their ancestral homelands in the Rocky Mountain foothills, the Comanches rolled southeastward in successive waves. Taming the descendants of tough Arab-Andalusian horses loosed by early Spanish settlers, they chased the buffalo astride their lathering backs. The Comanches' relentless fury finally compelled cowering tribes in southern Texas to call on the Spanish in Mexico to establish Texas missions as a barrier to the Comanches.

At Spain's extreme stretch north and the Comanches' farthest reach south the two peoples met in a bloody Texas standoff. At uneasy lancepoint they still faced each other when a third group, the American frontiersmen, strode into Texas in the 1820s. In these rugged interlopers the hard-riding warriors and hunters met their ultimate challenge and went down to bloody defeat.

Yet for two centuries the Comanches had reigned as western warlords in a singular explosion of cultural energy. More than barbaric horsemen, the Comanches shaped a sophisticated and admirable civilization which flourished in an often hostile land. Family, leadership, and livelihood they skillfully adapted to a mobile life, sweeping triumphantly over thousands of square miles of our now-American West.

The Comanches, who called themselves The People, split into five bands, and each molded its own distinctive life pattern around the ceaseless pursuit of the buffalo and other game. Allied in purpose and practice, these rough-hewn tribesmen created a remarkably vigorous culture almost unknown to Americans today. We remember the Comanches for their ferocity, their breathtaking riding skills, their courage—and fittingly so. But their accomplishments spanned far more than these warlike arts.

Preston Harper enlivens this hidden Comanche world through the story of his fictional heroes, Long Lance, Eagle, and Iron Bow of the Antelope band. Nomadic hunters had no time or inclination for books and letters, diaries and documents; their saga emerges from remnant bits of Comanche history, the lore and legend of times past. Yet in these stories based on real events and people, we see Comanche life not as it might have been, but as it really was. Comanche character and life, passion and pride come vibrantly and truthfully alive in the captivating story of the "Warlords of the West."

Dr. John Robinson, Chairman
Department of History
Abilene Christian University

C O M M A N C H E
C O U N T R Y

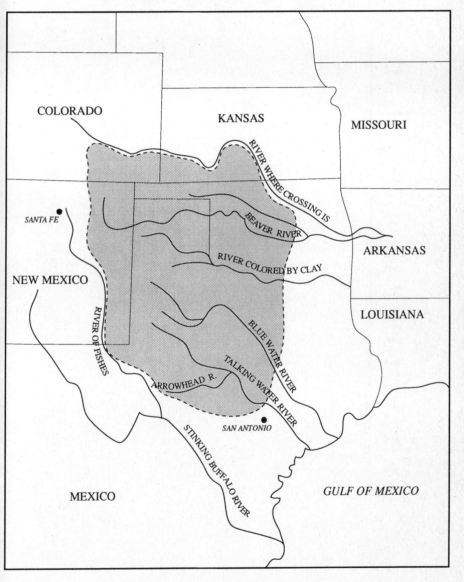

The House of Long Lance

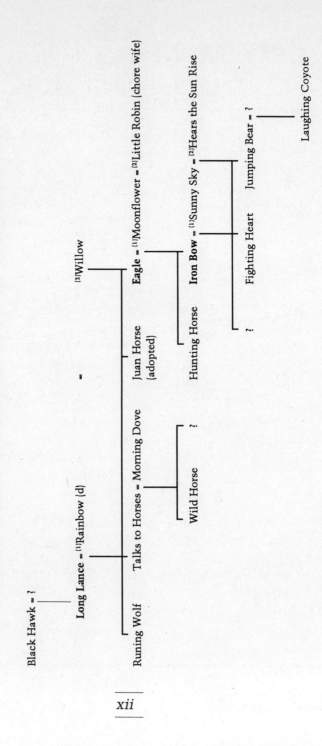

Black Hawk = ?

Long Lance = [1]Rainbow (d)

Runing Wolf

Talks to Horses = Morning Dove

[2]Willow

Wild Horse

?

Juan Horse (adopted)

Eagle = [1]Moonflower = [2]Little Robin (chore wife)

Hunting Horse

Iron Bow = [1]Sunny Sky = [2]Hears the Sun Rise

?

Fighting Heart

Jumping Bear = ?

Hears the Sun Rise

Laughing Coyote

THE WAR PARTY

PART 1:
GETTING READY

Long Lance sat at the fire in his tepee with five other Comanche chiefs of the Antelope band. They had just eaten copious amounts of buffalo and a delicious mush made from ground mesquite beans, buffalo marrow, and honey. After his wife, Willow, cleared away the bones and utensils, he picked up a long pipe with eagle feathers hanging from it and addressed the chiefs. "Long Lance has had a powerful vision."

The chiefs looked intently at their handsome, broad-shouldered host. Their rapt expressions gave no hint they already knew what the meeting was about and had probably made their decisions before coming. Long Lance was the most successful Antelope war chief in their memory. That his medicine was strong was no mere boast with him. He had proved it over and over, first with extraordinary individual heroics as a youth and then with brilliant leadership as he matured.

"Long ago the Antelope crushed the Apache like men fighting with children. Three times. Finally, the Apache moved into the mountains and desert toward the sunset." He lit and pulled strongly at the pipe. "This morning, Running Wolf returned with a hunting party that ranged as far as the River of Fishes." He puffed deeply and let the smoke out slowly. "There were many Apache tracks this side of the river. Running Wolf and another followed these tracks to the river. Just on the other side they saw wickiups and horses. Before they could learn more about this Apache, he saw them and chased them away."

Long Lance paused and looked into each chief's eyes before continuing. "Running Wolf believes there are at least two hundred warriors in the village." The other chiefs interjected grunts and groans of resentment. He held up a hand filled with light brown meal, letting it fall through his fingers. "In his vision Long Lance saw that the Great Spirit means for the Antelope to move at once and grind the Apache like mesquite beans." He crossed his arms on his broad chest and sat silently, giving his guests an opportunity to respond.

The other war chiefs sitting around the fire were Grey Cloud, Won the Race, Little River, and Buffalo Breath. Also present was the band's peace chief, Faster than a Horse. While he did not participate in the war parties anymore, he was invited because the others respected the older chief and his counsel. During his prime, he had been the principal war chief, as Long Lance was now; and because of the respect he had gained during his long, successful career, he became the peace chief. He was a big man with a craggy, scarred face and long unbraided silver hair.

Faster than a Horse spoke slowly; his voice sounded as though it came from a deep well. "Faster than a Horse has fought against the Apache and knows him well. He is like a coyote in his determination. If he is not stopped at once, he will band with our other enemies and try to take the Antelope's hunting grounds." He slammed a giant wrinkled hand to the ground. "He must be stopped!" He pointed at Long Lance. "For this war Long Lance is the one to lead."

The next oldest chief and the one second to Long Lance in popularity in the Antelope band was Grey Cloud. He had a broad pleasant face and deep-set eyes that wrinkled like dried figs at the corners when he smiled. He did not envy Long Lance's success; rather, he celebrated and promoted it. Grey Cloud was a courageous fighter and a generous and respected man, but he had the wisdom to know he lacked the military genius of Long Lance.

He said solemnly, "Grey Cloud has fought beside our great chief Long Lance in many battles. He is strong and fierce like the mountain lion, but he is also clever like the fox. Never has the Antelope had a greater leader. I thank the Great Spirit for sending him to us. Grey Cloud and his warriors will follow him anywhere." He looked defiantly at Buffalo Breath.

Buffalo Breath let out a derisive snort. He was a deep-chested man with a large head and small eyes. A knife scar ran along his left cheek from above his ear to the bottom of his jaw. "Grey Cloud will follow him to defeat!"

Won the Race and Little River regarded him with a mixture of respect and contempt. They knew he was jealous of Long Lance's success and felt he should be the principal war chief himself. He had recently led two successful war parties against the Ute, and his popularity was growing, especially with the younger warriors. The older warriors were still suspicious of him, however. He was bold but not clever. Unlike Long Lance, he often paid too high a price for victory. Bravery was to be admired, but there was not an unlimited supply of warriors.

Buffalo Breath puffed out his chest and snorted again. "Long Lance does not know this Apache as Buffalo Breath does. Buffalo Breath knew they were trespassing long before Long Lance did. My scouts have just returned from spying on this Apache. Buffalo Breath knows their location and numbers better than Long Lance does." He raised his eyes and looked toward the top of the tepee. "Among The People only Buffalo Breath has strong enough medicine to defeat the Apache."

The chiefs turned their eyes to Long Lance. He favored Buffalo Breath with a condescending smile. "Only a fool argues with a fool." He looked at the chiefs one at a time. "Or asks him to lead The People into war."

Seeing assent in their eyes, Long Lance passed his pipe and watched to see if any of the chiefs refused it. Grey Cloud smoked first and passed the pipe to Won the Race, who also smoked and passed it to Little River.

Little River, who was the youngest chief, hesitated. He had fought with Buffalo Breath against the Ute. He glanced at Buffalo Breath, and then he looked hard at Long Lance, studying his face. "Long Lance is the Antelope's strongest and greatest leader." Little River smoked the pipe and offered it to Buffalo Breath, who was bold but not stupid. He knew he would lose all his followers if he defied Long Lance. They would fight the Apache with or without him. He sighed deeply and took the pipe.

Long Lance nodded approval. "We must leave at once. Even now other tribes are watching this Apache's success. Unless they see our power, they will descend on us like grasshoppers on a summer prairie."

Moved by Long Lance's admonition and by the excitement of a war, the chiefs agreed on preliminary plans and then went straight to their tepees to make medicine. Long Lance sent a crier out into the village to spread the news and then went back into his tepee to make medicine—smoking, drumming, singing, and praying.

Soon all the village knew about the Apache menace and about the war party to be led by their greatest chief. Excitement was high, and the people, especially the women, busied themselves preparing for the war, though they would not be joining the men this time. Long Lance had indicated his plans for this raid would not permit the presence of women and children. Speed and secrecy would be of paramount importance.

The band was more excited than usual about this war. In addition to the ordinary desire to defend their hunting grounds, there was a deep hunger to confront the Apache. Some years earlier while Long Lance was on a raiding party in the south, his father, Black Hawk, led a war party against the Apache, who was no match for the Antelope on the plains. Black Hawk had made the mistake, however, of chasing the Apache into the mountains, where he proved to be a superior fighter. He killed Black Hawk and other great warriors. Afterwards, Long Lance led successful war parties and drove the Apache westward, but that first bitter defeat and the loss of family members had not faded from the memory of the band, though their names were never mentioned.

Long Lance had a farewell dinner in his tepee with Willow and their three sons, Running Wolf, Talks to Horses, and Eagle. Long Lance had painted his face black with red and blue decorative marks in preparation for the parades and war dance. His hair hung in braids over his chest, which bore a tattoo of a buffalo, the source of his medicine.

Willow was his second wife; his first, Rainbow, had been killed by the Apache when Long Lance was away; and after his time of grief, Willow came into his life and filled a great void. She was the only daughter and youngest child of Red Mountain. Having only one wife was unusual for a chief of Long Lance's stature. Most had three or more; however, the Great Spirit in a vision had forbidden polygamy for him; neither was he permitted to own slaves. Consequently, life was physically more difficult for Willow than for most wives.

Long Lance first noticed her two summers after Rainbow's death. He was returning from a raid to the north. When he rode into the village, he saw her running for water to put out a small grassfire beside her tepee. She was almost a head taller than most of the other women, and she ran gracefully with a long smooth stride. He had not seen many men run so well.

That same evening he visited Red Mountain's tepee and saw her again. Her eyes met his and warmed him with a special feeling. The next day he took a herd of fifteen choice horses to her tepee, and she immediately led them to mix with her father's herd. The marriage was made. As the years passed, she had proved a devoted wife and a successful mother to his two boys. Though she was older than Running Wolf by only ten winters, Willow helped to ease the pain Long Lance's sons felt at the tragic loss of their mother.

It happened when nearly all the Antelope warriors were away. Many of the best warriors had gone with Long Lance to fight the Ute when a small hunting party returned with the news that a Cheyenne raiding party was seen this side of the River Colored by Clay. Grey Cloud, who was in charge of the village, decided to take a war party to ambush the Cheyenne and drive him from The People's hunting grounds. Shortly after Grey Cloud's departure a large Apache hunting party came along and, finding the Antelope village poorly guarded, attacked at sundown. In the process of stealing a hundred horses, the Apache killed a dozen or more women and children who were tending them and carried off Rainbow with her two small sons; one was six and the other five.

Later that evening the boys were made to watch Apache warriors do terrible things to their mother. Then the warriors killed her and mutilated her body. During the night when an old warrior who was guarding the boys dozed off, they slipped away and hid in a grove of trees not far from camp. Two days later they were picked up by trackers sent out by Long Lance. He had just returned victorious from his war with the Ute. It turned out to be his saddest triumph.

Until Long Lance married Willow, Running Wolf nursed his hatred for the Apache and talked daily of completely destroying him. Talks to Horses, on the other hand, turned to animals for solace. He spent almost every waking hour with two Ute horses and a dog Long Lance had brought him. He trained the dog in a way that seemed beyond the power of a boy. With voice commands he could send the dog to fetch the horses, to take them past obstacles, to bring them to him, and to guard them all night.

Long Lance looked proudly at Talks to Horses and his other sons. He loved them and always before going to war arranged a farewell meal such as the one they had just completed. He had a special fondness for Eagle, Willow's only child. He had all the best qualities of both parents. He was tall and muscular, with striking good looks; and even as a child, he showed exceptional intelligence and courage. Long Lance knew he would one day be a great chief. His eyes passed to his oldest son, whose eyes were burning. "What is it, Running Wolf?"

"I want to fight in this war. I was one of those who discovered the Apache."

Long Lance was openly pleased with this young warrior, who had seen only seventeen winters. "Long Lance knew Running Wolf would want to go. All the best warriors want to go, and that is why he and some of the others must stay here. What happened in the past must not happen again. Running Wolf must stay here to protect his mother and brothers."

Running Wolf resisted the urge to argue with his father; it would be unmanly. On the other hand, Willow and the other sons were warmed by Long Lance's concern. He nodded and rose to leave. "This will be a bad war. If Long Lance does not return," he paused to look into each boy's eyes, "Live with honor and bravery." He embraced each of his family. Willow, who had an ominous feeling about this war, clung to her husband longer than she meant to. He put her gently away and held her at arm's length for a moment. Their eyes said what was in their hearts.

Just before sundown Long Lance stood on a knoll where he had spent a few last moments in prayer. He looked down on the hundreds of Antelope tepees grouped in a circle beside the Talking Water River. All his beloved people were making last minute preparations for the parade and the departure afterward. The river reflected the rich blue sky with faint streaks of orange. He breathed deeply of the mild spring air with its aroma of prairie flowers and smoked buffalo meat. He relished the distant sounds of barking dogs and neighing horses.

He hoped this would not be his last battle. He could not imagine that the Great Spirit's hunting grounds were better than this. He glanced at the sun beginning to sink into the hills. The Great Spirit had given The People this beautiful land with buffalo, deer, rabbits, birds, and other animals to live on. He drew in a deep breath. The People were strong and had many horses. No one—not the Apache, the Ute, the Spaniard—no one would ever be able to take this land from The People.

He thought of his handsome sons. Some day he would die in a battle, maybe this one. But he would live forever in them and in their sons after them. He lifted his arms in praise to Father Sun.

Before the sun disappeared from the horizon, the chiefs began the parades. The first to circle the village four times was Long Lance. As he rode, those who would follow him formed a procession behind. They were dressed in just breech-cloths, leggings, and moccasins. Their faces and bodies were painted, and each warrior carried a shield, a lance, or an ax.

Some warriors rode double, to indicate they had rescued fallen comrades in battle. As long as they lived, they knew they would be honored for their act of bravery. Many of the villagers who would not go on the raid walked alongside, cheering and joining in the war song of the raiders. The villagers who were most supportive expected to receive a horse or some other gift as a reward for their encouragement, if the war party returned victorious.

After Long Lance's parade, which had a hundred warriors, came the other four with about forty each. Plenty, they believed, to defeat the Apache, no matter how many warriors he sent out.

The War Dance followed the parades. For Long Lance it was the most magnificent of all the dances. Though there was no spiritual content—no attempt to raise a spirit of war—it was always enormously successful in building the warriors' enthusiasm for the raid and was at least partially responsible for the band's bravery and fierceness in battle.

Long Lance could not remember having heard the singers and drummers so loud as at this war dance. The fire in the middle of the village blazed higher than a tepee, and it seemed everyone was making noise. He was stirred with a deep devotion to his people combined with a thrilling urge to fight the battle now. When he made his entrance wearing his buffalo headdress and joined the dance, the noise rose to an even higher level.

After a long stint of vigorous dancing, Long Lance called for the chiefs to count coups. The drummers beat their drums with a low dramatic rhythm until Buffalo Breath halted them. Imitating the movements of a buffalo, he strode majestically into the middle of the circle and stood in front of the fire. He held up his battle ax. "Last winter Buffalo Breath led twenty warriors on a vengeance raid into Apache country. After his warriors had taken scalps, he led seventeen back home. Three more would not have come back except for this ax. They were to the rear and cut off by ten Apache warriors. Buffalo Breath saw it and rushed to their aid. Outnumbered ten to one, he swung this ax with the fierceness of a cornered wildcat. Four Apache warriors will never see the sun rise. The others turned their backs to Buffalo Breath and ran." The spectators cheered his account.

Buffalo Breath raised his hands as the ovation began to fade. "Great Spirit, you saw me do it. If I do not speak the truth, may my heart stop this night, and may I wander in eternal darkness." The dancers began again with boundless enthusiasm.

After several hours of dancing, and after chiefs and other popular warriors had counted coups, Long Lance walked into the circle and turned slowly to accept the thunderous ovation. He looked into the sea of painted faces and bodies, all of them cheering wildly; and he held up a clenched fist. The noise increased.

He raised the other arm to ask for silence. It took some time for everyone to quiet down. "For many winters now Long Lance has led raids against the Antelope's enemies, and he has seen great victories, almost as many as the stars in the sky." He pointed dramatically toward the darkened sky. "Long Lance and his warriors have fought the Ute, the Spaniard, the Osage, the Pawnee, the Tonkawa, and many more. None is more fierce and hateful than the Apache. He is a threat to the Antelope's village and his hunting grounds. The Antelope must tear him apart as the grizzly destroys the yapping dog." Deafening cheers burst out.

He waited several minutes and then held up his arms again. "Long Lance calls on all warriors to show the courage and skill in battle that will not only destroy the Apache but will also frighten away others who would dare intrude into this land of The People." He folded his arms across his chest, and accepted an ovation that did not stop until he signaled for the dances to continue. After a few he left, and the other chiefs began their departures.

PART 2:
THE BATTLE

Just after sunrise the war party assembled at a rendez-vous point below the mouth of Black Snake Creek. There, Long Lance gathered all the leaders into a circle around a large map drawn in the dirt. On the map he showed in detail all the important landmarks they would see during their four-day journey. He cut one notch in a sharpened stick and drove it into the ground at the end of the first day's journey and described the activities of that day. Similarly, he described the other three days, using sticks with the appropriate number of notches. Everyone, including Buffalo Breath, was given the opportunity to add information, and anyone who did not like the final plan was free to leave with all who shared his beliefs. Even Buffalo Breath grudgingly admitted the plan was brilliant. No one left.

Everyone traveled together until the fourth day; then Long Lance divided the war party into two groups. The first group, which he led, left in the morning and continued on a straight course for the Apache village. The second group, composed of one hundred and fifty warriors and led by Grey Cloud, left at noon and swung to the south before turning west toward the Apache. This group would not turn west until after midnight when the moon was high. Each group had a pair of scouts a half day's ride in advance.

Long Lance rode at the head of a hundred warriors with the sun at his back and the south wind lifting his braided hair. For him there was no feeling to equal the intoxication of leading men into war. It was the ultimate challenge, with life and indescribable joy to the victor and bitter pain and death to the loser. During war, men became like the Great Spirit—in control of life and death. He looked across the flat land that was green with grass and yellow with spring flowers. He inhaled the fragrance and let it escape slowly through his mouth.

Everyone's spirit was high throughout the day, and all held up lances and shouted toward sundown when they saw in the distance the low Dog's Teeth Mountains that marked the River of Fishes. Just across the river would be the Apache. Long Lance was sure they would not be able to surprise him. On such flat terrain the enemy should be able to see invaders for miles. Long Lance was counting on that; because if they were not observed, his plan would fail miserably. During the day he had been thinking about what to do in the unlikely event the Apache did not see his advance. A bloody retreat was the only possibility.

Raven's Wing rode to his side and pointed toward a distant mountain in the north, where a puff of smoke was rising into the white clouds. Long Lance nodded. "The Apache sees us."

Well after camp was made, the advance scouts returned with news that the Apache was preparing for war. Long Lance sent out two scouts at dusk. An hour later he sent out two more. It was unlikely the Apache would attack during the night, but he did not want to take a chance. He had trained himself always to be ready for the unexpected.

The warriors wore deer or buffalo hide shirts to protect them against the crisp desert air and sat in a large circle under a full moon. Long Lance permitted no fire tonight. He wanted the Apache to think the Antelope entertained the hope of an ambush. As they sat in the circle, they softly sang war songs and smoked from the sacred pipes they always brought to war. The final song before retiring was a prayer song to the Great Spirit, in which the leaders invoked his strength and protection for the coming battle.

The moon was high and bright when Goes Alone, one of the second pair of scouts, awakened Long Lance. "The Apache has killed Falling Tree and captured Horse's Rump." These were the first two scouts Long Lance had sent out.

"Where is Wolf's Friend?" asked Long Lance. He had been paired with Goes Alone.

"Just across the river. He watches the Apache."

"You have done well, Goes Alone. Ride back to the river. Stay on this side so you can bring news quickly if there is trouble."

Long Lance knew the Apache would be torturing Horse's Rump, and the thought brought new anxiety. He always took ability to withstand torture into consideration when he selected a scout, and Horse's Rump seemed tougher than most of the other young warriors. Still, one could never know. The Apache was more gifted than The People at torturing an enemy. Long Lance had heard of brave warriors turning into women when the pain became unbearable. Horse's Rump must hold out until the morning! If he gave in to pain and revealed Long Lance's plan, victory would go to the Apache. Long Lance marvelled that sometimes just one warrior could win or lose a war, no matter how strong or well prepared an invader was.

With the first light of dawn Long Lance led his brightly painted warriors at a gallop over the final twelve miles separating them and the Dog's Teeth Mountains. Despite the early morning chill, most wore only breech-cloths. Some wore pants made of deer or buffalo hide. Most wore feathers in scalp locks or small caps. Long Lance, Grey Cloud, and Buffalo Breath wore Buffalo headdresses. The warriors' principal weapons were bows and lances. Some carried battle axes instead of lances. Everyone had a knife at his side and a brightly decorated hide shield on one arm. Most of the horses were painted with marks and symbols, and feathers dangled from their tails and manes.

Long Lance slowed his warriors as they approached the path through the mountains. This was the hardest part, to ride deliberately into an ambush. He was not concerned for himself, even though he rode in front. He believed his medicine was so strong no weapons could harm him. He had concern for the others; he was leading some into certain death. He hoped the number to die would be minimized by a lack of discipline among the Apache.

The mountains were three hundred to five hundred feet high on either side of the pass, which was a good two hundred feet wide. This meant the Apache would be shooting at a distance that, when combined with a strong morning wind whipping in from the south, would cause some serious problems for the defenders. He thanked Mother Earth for the wind.

As almost always happened, even with the well-trained war parties of the Comanche, an overeager Apache fired a musket before the Antelope wariors were well into the pass. A shower of arrows and a few more musket balls followed. At least fifteen wariors fell from their horses. The others were holding up their shields to ward off most of the arrows. A dozen horses were thrashing around on the ground with arrows protruding from their necks or sides.

Long Lance ordered a retreat, but he stayed in the pass, holding up his shield as arrows continued to rain from the mountains. He rescued two horseless warriors and helped them find mounts. The bodies of the dead would have to wait for tomorrow. More than two hundred howling Apaches were storming down from the mountains, hungry to annihilate the outnumbered Antelope. They had on brightly colored head wraps and wore breech-cloths with buckskin shirts. Their moccasins came up to their knees. Some were shooting bows; others fired muskets they had gotten from the Spaniard. Most were brandishing clubs and spears. Like the Antelope warriors they had hide shields on one arm. Their screams were wild and eager. They could taste the sweetness of a great victory.

The retreat route was to the southwest through a small range of foothills, some no higher than a horse. During the night Grey Cloud had moved more than a hundred of his warriors into position to ambush the Apache from either flank as he rode through the hills chasing Long Lance. When the Antelope warriors approached the hills, Long Lance gave the signal for his army to divide into two previously arranged groups. Each group split again when it entered the hills, a seasoned warrior riding at the head of each group. The maneuver confused the Apache warriors, who also split up into smaller groups, but the groups were of unequal sizes, and some had ineffective leadership.

Confusion was complete for the Apache when Grey Cloud's party appeared and at pointblank range shot half the Apache warriors from their horses. Long Lance's warriors now swung back to attack the disoriented and badly outnumbered enemy. They used their favorite weapons to devastating effect, lancing the less agile Apache riders almost like buffaloes.

To complete the demoralizing of the Apache, smoke began to fill the sky over the river. In the night Buffalo Breath's warriors had moved up the river in position to strike when the Apache began to chase Long Lance. Now they had crossed the river and were razing the almost unprotected village, burning the wickiups and killing many of the surprised inhabitants. Some of the women and children would be taken for slaves.

By afternoon the Apache attack force had disintegrated. Two thirds were dead. The rest had retreated back into the hills where Long Lance, remembering the fate of Black Hawk, had forbidden pursuit.

PART 3:
COUNTING COUPS

Long Lance reassembled his forces at the previous night's campsite, where they were joined by Buffalo Breath's warriors. A knife-scarred but jubilant Horses's Rump rode at the front. His left ear was missing. All were eager to savor their victory and count coups. They had slaughtered almost a whole band and had about forty women and children whom they could either keep as slaves or trade to other bands for food and weapons. The captives, over five hundred horses, and much plunder from the village were assembled at the campsite.

For counting coups Long Lance and the other chiefs and leading warriors sat in a semicircle with a buffalo hide laid at the opening. Six drummers sat outside the circle, and at a signal from Long Lance began their stirring rhythms. Warriors began to dance spontaneously. The first to count a coup was Little River. He rode his brown and white horse into the circle, pulled up sharply, and rammed his lance into the buffalo hide. The music and dancers stopped.

Little River looked to the sun, "Father Sun, you saw me do this." Then he turned to Long Lance. "Early in the fight, before the Apache scattered, Little River saw two of them on the ground about to scalp Laughing Dog. Little River raced to his aid. The arrows flew by him like wind-driven sleet, and he had to fight through fifty spears. Little River plunged his lance into one of them and jumped from his horse with his knife against the other's spear. The Apache was no match. Even though Little River had only a knife, he would have killed the Apache easily except he was shot in the arm with this arrow as they fought." He lifted up a bloodstained arrow and held out his left arm to show a bloody buckskin bandage.

Little River continued, "Even with the arrow in his arm, Little River slit the Apache's throat and took his scalp." He held up the scalp for all to see and then pointed to an area where the wounded lay. "Laughing Dog lies yonder with an arrow wound in his side, but he will ride again to war. Little River brought him from under the Apache spear."

Before he spoke, Long Lance looked over at Grey Cloud, who nodded. "It was a mighty coup, Little River. Grey Cloud saw you do it. You have saved the life of a brave warrior and have brought great honor to yourself."

Because the battle was so bloody, it took the rest of the day and much of the night to count coups, especially since some warriors were involved in the same coup, and each wanted to tell his version. If one man shot an Apache from his horse, he received credit along with another warrior who was the first to touch the fallen Apache and shout, "Aiee!"

The celebration ended with a great feast made up of meats and other foods captured from the Apache village and prepared by the Apache women. Long Lance and most of the other warriors retired after the meal, since they had slept very little over the past few days. Long Lance did not pull his buffalo robe over him until he had spent time thanking the Great Spirit for this mighty victory over the Apache.

Warlords of the West

THE VISION QUEST

Eagle had seen thirteen winters and was eager to ride the warrior's road. He was now a skilled horseman, as good as most of the warriors, and he could shoot his bow with accuracy even while riding at full gallop. Though he had not attained full growth, he knew he had the strength and courage to become the kind of warrior his father would be proud of. He thought of Long Lance, his father, who was the greatest war chief of the Antelope band—the greatest of any Comanche band, so Eagle had heard.

All through the past winter his father had spent many hours working with Eagle, especially teaching him to use the lance, the favorite weapon of the Antelope. It was a weapon no man in memory had used so successfully as Long Lance. He was even reputed to have thrown it nearly a hundred paces and killed a Ute warrior who was stealing a favorite horse.

Eagle saw his father's lance lying beside his tepee. He hefted it, moving his hand forward on the shaft until he found the balance point. He remembered the first time he had lifted it two winters before. It had seemed heavy, and he could not throw it far. Eagle shifted into a throwing position, pointing it toward the warm afternoon sun. His arms and shoulders were muscular like a man's now, and he had a strong urge to throw the lance right into the sun.

"Will Eagle hunt birds with a lance?"

Eagle turned and looked up into the speaker's eyes. "Father, is Eagle not ready to ride the warrior's road?"

Long Lance's face was almost expressionless except for a sparkle in his eyes. He put his hands on his son's shoulders. "Yes, it is time to seek the vision and discover your source of power."

"Should Eagle ask Wounded Bear to guide him?" asked Eagle. Wounded Bear, the chief medicine man, had guided most of the youths through their vision experiences. Eagle knew, however, that Long Lance did not trust the medicine man anymore. Of late, his medicine was growing weaker, and Long Lance had twice accused him of sorcery.

Long Lance's eyes widened with anger. "Long Lance will guide you. His medicine is greater than Wounded Bear's." He sat beside the tepee and indicated Eagle should sit next to him. They said nothing for awhile, the autumn afternoon sun still warm on their naked shoulders.

"You will begin tomorrow morning. Before dawn go to the river. There, facing the rising sun, bathe thoroughly, cleaning your hair and every part of your body. Even though the water will be cold, you must do this carefully. It will be a purification of your body and your spirit." Long Lance looked toward the sun. "Father Sun will behold your purity and know you are ready to receive power."

"Where does Eagle go for his vision?"

"When you are out of the water, look to the east. Father Sun will show you where to go next."

"Should Eagle go straight to the place Father Sun shows him?"

"Yes. Along the way stop to smoke and pray four times. You must perform this ceremony four times each day that follows. Soon you will feel total harmony."

"When will Eagle receive his vision?"

"No one can say. If you do not receive one during the four days and you feel strong, stay one more day. If you still do not receive one, return home and try some other day." Seeing anxiety in Eagle's eyes, he placed his hands on the boy's shoulders. "Do not worry. You will receive a vision. Long Lance has prepared you himself. Eagle is ready."

Eagle was still uneasy. "Why do some not receive visions, and some, only weak ones?"

"They are not ready in their spirits to take on strong medicine, or they do not have a guide with strong medicine." Long Lance studied the horizon. Brilliant colors were forming as the sun began to set. "The last two boys Wounded Bear sent out did not receive visions, even though everyone thought they were ready."

"Is that all?" He sensed his father wanted to say more.

"It is hard for boys to go four days without food and water." Long Lance looked into Eagle's eyes. "You must do it. Do not surrender to your body's demands. Also, remember your ceremonies, and sleep with your head covered with your buffalo robe. Always sleep with your feet to the east so when you rise in the morning, you will look into the sun. Father Sun will renew your spirit as food renews a starving body."

"Why must Eagle sleep with his head covered?" Eagle rubbed his arms. The air had chilled as the sun began to disappear.

"The medicine of the buffalo will keep away evil spirits of the night." Long Lance rose to indicate the conference was ended.

"I will say goodbye." Eagle turned toward his mother's tepee.

"No, Willow is at a time when you should not go to her. Tonight you will eat and sleep in the tepee of Long Lance. He will help you make further preparations for your journey."

After a meal of roasted venison, sent by Willow, the boy and his father discussed the coming adventure; and Eagle's excitement grew. When it was time to sleep, he could not. He lay in the dark and reflected on his past life as a carefree boy. He was thinking how that would change into the exciting life of a warrior. He visualized himself fighting heroically against Utes, Apaches, Tonkawas, and other enemies of his band. Fantasy led to fantasy until a restless sleep finally came in the early morning.

Long Lance woke him when the first light of dawn touched the sky. Eagle quickly assembled his pipe, tobacco, and material to light it with. These he carried in a small deerskin pouch. His only other baggage was his buffalo robe, which he rolled tightly and tied across his back. He took a long drink of water and accepted his father's hand in farewell. "The Great Spirit will be with you," Long Lance assured him.

Wearing nothing but a breech-cloth and moccasins, he was tempted at first to wrap the buffalo robe about him. Frost was on the grass, and long puffs of vapor formed with his breathing. Instead, he jogged a few minutes until his body warmed from within. Then, it felt good to have the cold air biting at his skin. He wanted to feel everything as intensely as possible.

"Now Eagle is a man," he thought. "Pain and discomfort will never again make him whine or cry like a child or a woman." Still, he jogged some more, even though his father had warned him to conserve his energy. He convinced himself he was doing this to show Father Sun he was eager to begin worshipping him.

As the village was near the Talking Water River, Eagle arrived at the water before the first rays of sun began to warm it. It was grey and looked cold, but he was cheered by the sight of two rabbits running for the cover of brown grass. "Eagle is greater and stronger than the animals," he thought.

He sat beside the river and prayed until the rim of the sun began to send warming rays; then he walked slowly into the chilly water. He had to gasp for breath as his upper body was immersed, yet he did not rush. He moved deliberately, the way he had seen religious rituals performed. The awareness of cleansing and the transition to manhood warmed him and made the bath refreshing. As he came up from the water, the sun's rays felt as warm as on a midsummer's day and gave him a feeling of inner strength and great physical energy. He was almost oblivious to the morning breeze that chilled his wet skin.

After walking about two miles east of the river, he sat facing the sun and ceremoniously lit his first pipe of tobacco, which he understood to have both medicinal and mystical properties. He was sitting at the edge of a grove of giant live oak trees where the birds were chirping and the squirrels were chattering. Because frost was still on the grass, he had to strike his flints against moss he had brought in his pouch. After the soothing smoke he prayed: "O, Great Spirit, look with favor on Eagle, who now comes seeking power. Show him where to go. Favor him with attention and accept him as one who will be a great warrior and bring glory to The People."

After praying he looked a mile to the east and saw an eagle swoop down for its prey on a large bluff called Hump of the Buffalo. It stood boldly against the morning sky, as massive as the animal from which it took its name. It was an ideal location for a vision, and Eagle was sure Father Sun meant him to go there. The bluff would be eminently suitable because of the grand view from the top and because it was only two hours' walk from the village. His father had talked of the danger of going too far, since he would be weak from hunger and thirst when the time came to return.

He stopped three more times to smoke and pray before he reached the bluff, arriving at noon. Accustomed to eating a big meal at noon, he felt a raging hunger, and he was thirsty from the walk and the smoking. Far from discouraging him, these discomforts inspired him, making him feel the spiritual magnitude of his task. His father had often told him the mark of a warrior with great medicine is his enormous capacity for pain and suffering.

Eagle knew he must learn to let spiritual food and water sustain him for long periods of time—weeks if necessary. His grandfather, Red Mountain, had told him of a time the Antelope migrated during a drought. The men drank only a mouthful of water a day so the women and children would have enough. By the time they reached water, their lips were clotted with blood, and their throats were swollen shut. Several warriors died, but none complained. Eagle imagined himself one of the warriors and was inspired by the fantasy.

He had climbed the bluff before and so knew the way, reaching the top by mid-afternoon. His main interest was seeing the sky and the plains below; and since there were no trees and hardly any other kind of vegetation in the rocky soil, he did not have to worry about an obstructed view. For his camp site he chose a comfortable position on the south side from which he could see to the horizon in all directions.

At first, he was awed by the view and the circumstances of his being there; however, lightheaded from the unaccustomed hunger, he dozed through the late afternoon, not waking until brought to consciousness by the stillness and slight change of temperature when the sun began to set.

Rested by his light sleep and inspired by the dazzling red and orange colors of the sunset, he carefully lit his pipe and sat meditatively gazing at the heavenly spectacle. For the first time in his life he felt the presence of the Great Spirit fused with the earth, the sun, and with his own spirit. Because the experience was so intense, he thought there might soon be an accompanying vision.

There was no vision, and as darkness enfolded him, the spiritual intensity faded. He grew anxious. He was, after all, only a boy away from home for the first time. Perhaps the Great Spirit had more important persons to take care of.

Eagle drew his robe about him and prayed a prayer his father had instructed him to say: "Great Spirit, maker of the sun, the moon, the stars, and the earth; giver and taker of life, hear Eagle, who comes seeking power. Accept him and favor him with powerful medicine. With this medicine he will do good and never evil. He will be a great warrior and protect his people. He will always keep the tribal laws and be just with others." Praying soothed his spirit, and he fell asleep almost as soon as he ended the prayer, being sure first to cover his head with the buffalo robe.

Each day he would follow the same routine. He would rise early to face the morning sun and try to be meditative and prayerful through the day, especially as he performed his ceremonies.

His spirits were high the second morning; he felt grown up and close to the Great Spirit. He sensed the Spirit's presence in everything and was indifferent to physical discomfort. When he looked to the east, he felt as though he were pure spirit, able to soar over the rugged plains like the eagle whose name he bore. When he saw warriors leave camp, he was filled with a sense of oneness with them. Soon he would ride with them as an equal. The thought brought an even greater spiritual intensity, but he was disappointed with the afternoon. He was not so successful with his meditations as he thought he would be. His hunger distracted him, and he had a burning desire to ride, to hunt, and to be with other people.

That night he slept restlessly; and though he prayed often, he felt abandoned by the Great Spirit. By midafternoon of the next day, his thirst was unbearable. His fervent prayers seemed trite, falling upon his ears with a harsh grating sound like stones grinding corn. The more he tried to recover his earlier mystical awareness, the more alone he felt. He feared the Spirit had examined him and found him lacking in some area.

"No!" he shouted. "Eagle will not accept that. He is the son of the great Long Lance." He pounded his chest with his fists. "Long Lance said Eagle is ready. Speak to him, Great Spirit. Give him a vision." He stood waiting for a long time looking toward the sun, and then sank wearily to his knees and tried another prayer.

He was deeply depressed that night. Nothing was happening. He would have to go home in the morning a failure. His father would be disappointed but understanding. The other boys would tease him, especially the ones who had received their vision the first time they sought it.

A strong, freezing wind blew in from the north as he lay tossing fitfully in the darkness on the hard, unfriendly ground. The hours passed with the slowness of a cat stalking its prey. Then, sometime in the early morning just before sunup, the wind stopped.

The vision came clearly and magnificently as when Father Sun disperses the storm clouds with blinding light and brilliant colors. It was filled with sweetness and freshness like a prairie morning after a thunderstorm. He heard the lark sing, and he saw a giant buck with many-pointed antlers standing by a river—it looked like the Talking Water River. On the shore were delicious-looking bowls of some of his favorite foods, like ground mesquite beans mixed with buffalo marrow and topped with honey. The buck avoided them all, passing to the other side of the river where he examined fresh meat from a buffalo and several other animals. The meats were garnished with pecans and other wild fruits and nuts. The buck ate heartily of these and then, with his antlers lowered, he raced across mountains and plains killing Apaches, Utes, Spaniards, and other enemies of The People.

Four times that morning Eagle prayed and smoked his pipe, thankful for the Great Spirit's bountiful gift. In the early afternoon he descended the mountain, full of excitement and anticipation. He especially wanted to visit the river, though he knew deer rarely went there before evening.

At the river he drank deeply and then lay on the bank to soak his tired feet in the cool water and warm his chest with the afternoon sun. As he was about to leave, the largest buck he had ever seen sprang from a grove of live oaks and crossed the river about a hundred and fifty paces downstream. On the other side he joined a couple of other bucks, and they ran into the woods.

Those who saw Eagle were surprised when he ran into camp. They suspected he had been eating and had not pursued his vision correctly. Long Lance made no comment but took him into his tepee and smoked his pipe while Eagle ate a big buffalo steak Willow prepared for him. Afterwards, Eagle carefully and reverently related all he had done and seen. His father remained silent, showing no signs of pleasure, though Eagle knew it was there.

"It was a strong vision," responded his father at the conclusion of Eagle's account. "The Great Spirit has shown special favor. Some day Eagle will be a great warrior unless he betrays his power."

"Never!" exclaimed Eagle.

"It is hard to own such strong medicine. You must live with some difficult taboos." Long Lance looked hard at Eagle for dramatic effect. "Bucks are now big medicine for you, and you must never eat them or any of the things you saw the buck avoid before crossing the river."

"The mesquite bean mush is delicious," Eagle said sadly.

"You will have to eat fruit when you desire sweetness." Long Lance then enumerated taboos, some common to all warriors, like protecting his medicine by avoiding cooking grease, sick people, and women during their menstrual periods.

Regarding the rest of Eagle's vision, Long Lance warned, "Being a leader requires great courage and dedication. There will be many sacrifices to make." He placed a hand on Eagle's shoulder. "If Eagle cannot live with all this, he will have to climb the bluff again and return the medicine."

Eagle rose and crossed his arms on his chest. "Eagle will never return his power. He will be a great chief like his father."

3

THE WHITE
BUFFALO

It was a successful buffalo hunt, the first Running Wolf had led. He had directed a swift maneuver from upwind of this immense herd. Within minutes the Comanche hunters had closed a portion of the herd into a tight group so they could kill the buffaloes without running them hard. This way the meat would not be hot and spoil quickly when the women butchered it on this warm autumn day. The hunters were working with swiftness and precision. They had already killed over a hundred of the big grunting, heaving animals; and the women were moving in to help clean them. Everything was going perfectly; soon the hunt would be over, and they could celebrate.

Eagle, having killed enough animals for one day, sat on his horse, Lightning, and took in the spectacle. The buffalo herd stretched almost to the horizon, and with their shaggy winter coats they blended in with the frost-killed grass and the leafless trees that dotted the plains. Only a few of the

hunters were still killing. Eagle's eye caught his brother
Running Wolf riding at full gallop in pursuit of one of the
buffaloes some distance ahead. He was a handsome, graceful warrior with a strong resemblance to his father. The
muscles along his back and shoulders bulged as he bent
forward, urging his blue and white horse along. Eagle
kicked the flanks of Lightning, a big yellow stallion with
black mane and tail.

In a moment Eagle could see Running Wolf was after the
leader, a gigantic white buffalo the Antelope band called
Piatosa. Piatosa had turned all the cows into the middle of
the herd, and he stood majestically and defiantly apart,
snorting and pawing the ground. His mammoth head was
held slightly downward so that his horns were in the thrust
position. The horns were longer than Eagle had ever seen on
a buffalo. He could easily gore a man to death with them.

Piatosa had been seen numerous times over the past few
years, and legends had grown about him. Wounded Bear, the
chief medicine man, had treated wounds inflicted by Piatosa, and he claimed the animal was, in fact, an incarnation
of Father Sun. He warned all hunters to leave him alone.
Long Lance had scoffed at this and other stories but said he
had avoided killing the animal himself because so many of
The People thought he was taboo.

Running Wolf had told Eagle he would one day kill
Piatosa so the tribe would see how great his own medicine
was. A number already felt Running Wolf was in some ways
as great as his father because of the successful war party he
had just participated in against the Ute far to the north. His
warriors had taken many scalps and brought back a hundred
horses laden with jewelry, weapons, and furs. Eagle had
longed to go, but Long Lance had a rule that the two
brothers could not go to a war together.

Running Wolf circled Piatosa, pretending he was interested in another animal, and the white buffalo bent to sniff the grass. Eagle recognized what Running Wolf was planning. In killing a buffalo with a lance, it was best to come in from the rear and thrust the lance downward between the hipbone and the ribs. Running Wolf sat quietly for a few minutes while Piatosa grazed; then he slowly moved closer to the big animal. When he was thirty paces from him, Running Wolf lowered his lance and raced in for the kill.

Eagle was frozen; unable to move, as he watched events unfold like a bad dream. He was amazed at the big animal's quickness—he moved more like a big cat than a buffalo. As the lance came near, Piatosa pivoted. Running Wolf's horse was startled by the move and shied just slightly. The two actions caused the lance to miss its mark, sticking instead into the hump.

Holding tenaciously to his lance, Running Wolf was jerked from his horse and thrown to the ground. Stunned, he rose slowly to his feet. Too slowly. Before Running Wolf could escape, Piatosa knocked him to the ground and trampled him. He then trotted proudly toward the setting sun, and the rest of the herd started in behind. If Running Wolf had survived Piatosa's hoofs, he was dead now.

Eagle was filled with rage, and desire for revenge burned through his body with each beat of his pounding heart. He leaned forward and violently kicked the sides of his horse.

"Wait, Eagle!" The voice belonged to Fought until the Moon Came Out, Eagle's closest friend. He rode alongside Eagle and grabbed the yellow horse's reins. "You must be patient! You can do nothing now!"

As his horse slowed, Eagle realized his friend was right. Piatosa was gone, and he would have to live with his anger and his pain awhile. He blinked back tears of frustration and sorrow. He remembered how he and his brother only a few hours earlier were proud to be sons of Long Lance riding together in the fall hunt.

In the Antelope village the next day, Eagle sat at a fire with Wounded Bear and the peace chief, Grey Cloud. Wounded Bear crossed his arms on his sagging chest and spoke gravely. "The white buffalo is a spirit. He cannot be killed. Wounded Bear told Running Wolf this. If he had listened, he would be alive today. Now he is dead and cursed forever for offending a spirit."

Grey Cloud looked without expression into the fire. Then he nodded his head.

Eagle wished Long Lance were here instead of on a raid. His father would make Wounded Bear and the rest of the band know the truth. Instead, he had to speak for his brother; and because he had not done many great deeds yet, his words would be given little respect. "Long Lance said all animals are a gift to man. Unless they are a personal taboo, it is right to kill them for food and clothing. The buffalo was not a taboo for Running Wolf. He had a right to kill Piatosa." He stood, indicating his unwillingness to hear more. "Eagle believes this."

Wounded Bear was relishing what he saw as his moment of victory. Running Wolf had tried to undermine his influence and had paid for it with his life. Now everyone would respect Wounded Bear's words without questioning. No one would listen to an untried youth like Eagle. He lifted his wrinkled arms to the sky and spoke loudly, as if to hold the younger warrior with his voice. "Running Wolf offended the Great Spirit when he attacked the white buffalo. He will never enter the Great Spirit's hunting grounds."

Eagle controlled his anger and looked into the old man's eyes. "Wounded Bear is mistaken. Eagle will bring back the head of the white buffalo." He spread his arms dramatically. "All The People will know my father spoke the truth and my brother is already with the Great Spirit." Without waiting to talk even to Fought until the Moon Came Out, Eagle gathered provisions and set out on Lightning to find the white buffalo.

Weeks later, after searching miles of grassy plains, watching at every known water hole, and observing four herds, Eagle came to the biggest herd yet. It was an unusually warm day for winter, much like the day his brother died, Eagle reflected. There was little wind; and the sky was a bright, hard blue. He leaned forward on his yellow horse and shielded his eyes from the sun. The old medicine man's hated words echoed in his mind as he strained to see the leader, trying to distinguish the colors. He could not go home without the white buffalo's head, even if he had to spend all winter and the next spring hunting.

The herd was so large he had to ride almost an hour to get close enough to see the leader clearly. When the herd swung toward the west, the leader moved a little ahead; and the sunlight hit squarely on his back. The animal's coat was longer and whiter than when Eagle had seen it before, but he was sure. It was Piatosa. Eagle was filled with a mixture of awe and hatred for this animal that had killed his brother. The emotion was stronger than he realized, having been fed by weeks of anger and frustration. He reached down and gripped his lance tightly. Piatosa must die by the lance.

He nudged the yellow horse, and they raced toward the white buffalo. He was inspired by more than anger now. It was the thrill of the hunt, a feeling he had thought would never come again after seeing his brother trampled by

Piatosa. This feeling even exceeded others he had felt. It was as though he were facing something more than an animal, more, even, than a man, yet Eagle did not let the thrill destroy his self-control. This was the confrontation he had been seeking; he must not do anything stupid and miss his chance to exonerate his brother. He made a wide loop around the front of the grazing herd and approached from the south with the wind in his face.

When he approached, he pulled back on the reins, riding slowly as though he were casually passing by; and since he was quiet and did not kill any of the herd or interfere with their eating, they disregarded him. Then Piatosa, with an uncanny sense of danger, knew he was there and began to run back toward the north with the herd picking up speed behind him. Eagle was neither surprised nor alarmed. His horse was much faster than the buffaloes, and he moved past hundreds of them. For awhile he forgot about his brother and the medicine man, and he felt one with his horse as their spirits were caught up in this thrilling chase that must end in death.

As Eagle approached the front of the herd, he realized he would not be able to get close enough to Piatosa to use his lance. The animal had a virtual bodyguard around him. And trying to work his way through the frightened herd could prove disastrous. He might be trampled as his brother was. With these realizations came the fear he might never see the white buffalo again. What if the herd ran all night and somehow Piatosa escaped? The buffaloes were fresh, and his pony was tired after a day of riding and chasing. It had been hours since he had watered the horse.

Remembering his brother's death, Eagle drew an arrow and fitted it to his bow. Piatosa was much larger than the other buffaloes; and though not much of his head was visible, his hump made a fair-sized target for Eagle, who from the start of his training had been an exceptional shot from his pony. He released the arrow and watched it ricochet off Piatosa's hump. It was as though the arrow had struck a rock. He shot another arrow. This one hit lower and struck in the animal's hide, though it flopped about, having done little if any harm. However, it seemed to infuriate him, and the run soon developed into a stampede. Eagle dropped back and followed the herd until well after dark, when it stopped at the Blue Water River. After watering his thirsty horse and eating the last of his supply of jerked buffalo meat, Eagle wrapped up in a blanket made from the hide of a buck, his source of power. It gave him good protection against the cold winter air but did not calm his troubled spirit.

Sleep would not come to release him from his fatigue and anxiety. He sat up and took the small medicine bag from around his neck and took out four buck's teeth. He held them in his hand and sang songs to the Great Spirit. Before long he felt relaxed and was able to drop into a light sleep. Throughout the remainder of the night he tossed about with dream after dream. In some he saw his brother die; in others he saw himself trampled by Piatosa. Finally, toward dawn, he had a radiant vision of Running Wolf riding a beautiful white horse across a green plain lancing white buffaloes. Then he had a few moments of peaceful sleep— enough to refresh his strong, young body.

He arose quietly as soon as there was enough light to move around without stumbling. Since Piatosa was a special animal, Eagle would use special techniques to kill him. Moving quickly, he plunged his lance into the heart of a small bull sleeping at the perimeter of the herd. Deftly, he sliced and stripped away the hide, leaving the head attached. Soon he had the costume he needed to move among the herd without causing another stampede. It was a technique he had seen used by his father during their first hunt together.

The herd was moving about as Eagle finished his preparations. He must act quickly now. He threw the still clammy skin over his body and moved on all fours to the front of the herd. The danger was great. The herd was still jittery from the stampede of the previous night, and Piatosa would probably be unusually alert. If he started another stampede, Eagle would be trampled.

When he reached his destination, Eagle understood why his disguise had worked so well. Piatosa's attention was occupied by another big bull, which had challenged his right to lead. The two animals stood heads down fifty feet apart, snorting and pawing the ground. The ceremony completed, they thundered toward each other and butted heads with a terrific thud. The noise shattered the morning air like a great clap of thunder, reverberating among the distant hills. After the impact, the challenger staggered a moment on wobbly legs and then ran back into the herd. Piatosa stood alone, his head lifted proudly as if to beckon other challengers. Seeing none, he paraded triumphantly so all might behold his eminence.

Piatosa in his pride was not alert to danger. Eagle moved beside an admiring group of cows and stood crouched, his lance ready. As the great white beast paraded by, favoring the cows with his special attention, Eagle jumped forward and thrust his lance into Piatosa's side. The buffalo was a third bigger than any Eagle had attacked before, and his hide seemed almost as tough as the shields the Antelope made from weathered and beaten skins. Also, it had been extremely difficult to get a good angle. He had come directly from the side instead of from the rear, and he had been standing instead of sitting high on his horse. Because he was strong and his lance had a metal point, the weapon had gone in but not deeply enough to kill. In fact, it appeared to have no ill effect.

The great bull bellowed with rage and turned abruptly on the young warrior, jerking the lance from his hand and sending him sprawling on the trampled-hard ground. If he had been on a horse, Eagle might have suffered the same fate as his brother. Instead, he leapt to his feet clutching his long metal hunting knife, a trophy from a raid on the Spaniard. He looked around. The herd had pulled in around him to watch the fight. Some seemed even to be laughing at him. He had heard older warriors say buffaloes had laughed at and talked to them.

Eagle was confident in his fighting skills; he had fought with enemy warriors, some older and more experienced than he, but none proved to be as strong or as quick. This confidence in his skills almost cost him his life. He waited too long. The animal was even quicker than he remembered. Piatosa caught Eagle's left hip with one of his long horns and hurled him a good ten feet–before the young warrior could make a stab with the knife.

As Eagle struggled to his feet, blood flowing from the gash in his hip, Piatosa was almost on top of him again. This time, however, he was moving noticeably slower, and Eagle saw blood had saturated his left side below the lance, and there was a bloody froth on his mouth.

Eagle's hip burned like fire and refused to support his weight. When Piatosa approached, all Eagle could do was roll over, avoiding the deadly hoofs. The furious animal saw his assailant was injured and slowed the next charge, coming in with head down. Eagle spun as he rolled and deftly plunged his knife into the buffalo's belly. The maneuver left his body vulnerable to Piatosa's hoofs, however, and a rear hoof caught him in the back. Because he was rolling, Eagle did not catch the full weight of the buffalo, but the blow was still powerful enough to turn everything black.

He lay heaving, trying to get his breath, trying not to be sick. Somehow he must get ready for the next attack. He must not die. He pulled himself to his knees, swept by waves of nausea. Never had he felt pain like the pain in his back. Through the darkness in his head, Eagle could barely see Piatosa. The animal kept coming in and out of focus so that Eagle could not gauge his distance accurately. He guessed about two of the animal's body lengths. The knife and the spear still protruded from his body, and he was heaving loudly. In the background Eagle could see a fog of buffalo faces and bodies.

Piatosa lowered his head for a charge. Eagle strained to regain his feet. He could not move. Now he knew he would die, and he felt a great sadness. Wounded Bear was right. Piatosa was a spirit, and he had offended a spirit. He and his brother would suffer forever. His father and mother would know double the shame he had wanted to save them from. He made another effort to rise but instead toppled awkwardly to his side, still facing Piatosa. The pain was burning his whole body, and unconsciousness was taking control.

Using all his energy, Eagle forced his eyes to remain open, and he rose on his right elbow. He refused to receive death with closed eyes. This realization of imminent death cleared his head, and he could see more clearly than ever before. He

could even see the red veins in the eyes of the enraged white
buffalo. He could see the tiny white bubbles of froth that
drooled from his mouth.

Piatosa sprang forward with enormous power. Clearly,
he relished the death of this two-legged animal that, like
others before him, had foolishly defied his great power.

Eagle braced to receive the blow as the animal lowered
his horns for the kill. It never came. The animal plunged to
the ground only a few feet in front of Eagle. Something
inside must have exploded with that final great surge.

With enormous effort Eagle turned to face the herd. It was
already moving back to the south, following the bull that
had been defeated only moments earlier by Piatosa.

Eagle took a deep breath and lay back on the grass, lifting
his arms in thanksgiving to Father Sun. Tomorrow or the
next day he would ride back into the Antelope village with
the head and the hide of the white buffalo tied to his horse.
His first visit would be to the tepee of Wounded Bear.

THE MUSTANG

Talks to Horses watched a small herd of mustangs watering at the Blue Water River. From his vantage point atop a tree-covered hill that sloped down to the river, he could see the entire herd. It consisted of the leader, a big black stallion, and thirty mares. He wanted the beautiful stallion. It was not the beauty alone that would make the animal a valuable possession, however. The horse showed exceptional intelligence along with great strength, endurance, speed, and quickness. He was the kind of wild horse a warrior might hope to find once in ten years. Talks to Horses had a white mare he called White Wind that had, to a lesser degree, all these same qualities.

"What magnificent colts they will make!" he whispered to his horse, Honey, so named because of its color. Talks to Horses thought excitedly of several other mares besides White Wind he would also mate with the black stallion.

He had already hunted this mustang, which he called Night Wind, longer than any he had ever caught before, and he sometimes wondered if he would ever catch him. This might be his last chance. He had recently agreed to go down below the Stinking Buffalo River on an extended raid with his younger brother, Eagle. They would be gone all summer; and when he returned, the fine black mustang might be gone—would almost certainly be gone. Just the thought of not catching the pony brought sadness. He had never ridden Night Wind, never even touched him; but he loved him.

Talks to Horses reflected a moment on the raid to Mexico. It would be filled with beauty. They would cross vast ranges covered with deep, green grass and colorful wild flowers. He would see hills and mountains and cross cool, blue streams and rivers. After they crossed the Stinking Buffalo River, there would be arid land, which also had a special kind of beauty. He especially liked the early morning and the sunsets of the desert. Also, he would see many kinds of birds and animals, perhaps a few he had not seen before. The other warriors would ride quietly, concentrating on the raiding and killing to come. He would also ride quietly. The difference would be that his spirit would be feeding minute by minute on the bounty Mother Earth provides. When the time came to raid and kill, he would participate. That was expected of him as a warrior; but it was the beauty, not the violence, he looked forward to.

He wiped sweat from his brow with the back of his hand. It was the hottest day of the year, just the kind of day he had been hoping for. As he studied the horses, he thought of another hot day many summers back when he was only a boy. His father, Long Lance, was away on a raid when the Apache struck the Antelope village. He was tending horses with his mother and his older brother, Running Wolf.

Frantically, his mother grabbed them and told them to run and hide among the trees at the Talking Water River. The Apache caught them before they got there. Time would never remove his horrible memories of that evening and what the Apache did to his mother. Tears came to his eyes as he thought of his gentle mother.

Running Wolf, from the day Rainbow died, thought continuously of becoming a warrior so he could get personal revenge on the Apache. Until he died under Piatosa's hoofs, his hatred burned in him like a smoldering fire in a giant oak tree and could not be extinguished by any amount of killing. He lived to kill—not just the Apache, but all enemies of the Antelope. Talks to Horses, on the other hand, was repelled by the violence. He found balm for his pain in Mother Earth.

She taught him how to find peace. He became a close observer of plant and animal life, learning all the flowers in Comanche country, along with where and when they grew. He explored the rivers and creeks and climbed nearly every mountain.

Others thought his solitary expeditions were merely for hunting and often chided him for being such a poor hunter, since he rarely returned with game. When he did kill, the animals had usually been wounded or crippled by someone or something else. For food he preferred fruits and nuts to animal flesh.

He ignored the chiding. His happiness did not depend on the good opinion of the other warriors. But it had bothered Running Wolf. He sometimes insisted on joining Talks to Horses in his explorations so he could kill game to bring back and silence the jeers. The game was not what produced the silence, though. It was Talks to Horses' expertise at horse breeding and horsemanship. Taking care of his father's large herd, he had seen only sixteen winters when he began breeding and training the finest of Antelope war ponies.

His horse-breeding efforts also drew jeers at first. In the Antelope band the women took care of the horses, and they did well; but they did not have the understanding and skills Mother Earth had given him. The jeers were mild; no one wanted to risk the wrath of Long Lance. Besides, his expertise was soon apparent to everybody, and no one appreciated excellence in horses more than The People. A good horse was often the difference between life and death.

His study of nature led to other skills unusual in one so young. His bows and arrows were without exception the finest made by any warrior in the band. Most of the bow makers were old warriors who no longer went to war. They made good bows but not so good as his. Although they had time, most did not have the skill and the eye for detail Talks to Horses had. Perhaps of most importance, he had an exceptional ability to select the finest trees for his bows, using only the best bois d'arc or hickory. And there was another factor—love. He loved the wood and learned its qualities, treating each bow as an individual, almost as a close friend. Others made bows in three or four days; he took a month or more sometimes and produced a beautiful work, highly polished and excellent in every way. His wooden bows surpassed in quality and beauty all the horn bows he had seen, and they were so highly prized that he could have almost any maiden or horse he wanted in exchange for one.

One could not trade for such a rare horse as Night Wind, though. He watched the horse holding his head up sniffing the air, as though he sensed danger. Talks to Horses was sure the animal could not smell him. The day was windy, and he was downwind. The horse was careful by nature. "That is why you have remained free so long," mused Talks to Horses. Slowly, Night Wind walked to the water and put his head down. "Drink deeply," whispered Talks to Horses.

The first time he had tried to capture Night Wind, he had used the technique most often used by the Comanche. It was the previous fall. Because a scout had reported where the herd was, Talks to Horses was able to make careful preparations. He assembled two groups with himself as leader of one and Eagle as leader of another.

His own group hid about a mile from where the herd was grazing, and Eagle's stampeded it toward them. Talks to Horses and his group raced out when the horses came near and tried to lasso the best ones, but Night Wind and some of the other fastest ones were too quick for them. The horses they captured were good for trading with other bands, but not for use in war.

The next attempt came in the winter when the grass was less plentiful, and the horses became thinner and weaker than normal. Talks to Horses and a dozen other warriors found Night Wind with a large herd moving south. Riding their well-fed horses, they pursued the herd a full day. Many of the wild mustangs became weary and dropped back. They were captured. Night Wind led the faster horses beyond the horizon.

In the spring he organized another party to hunt the wild mustangs. He knew they, like other herds, tended to run in a great circle when pursued. This time each warrior brought along an extra mount. They intended to ride two days if necessary. He smiled faintly, thinking about the chase. True to form, the mustangs ran in a great circle; so to minimize their own efforts, the warriors rode on the inside of the circle, changing horses frequently. Unfortunately, they had ridden two hard days to catch the herd, and even though they could still catch normal horses, Night Wind escaped. It was the warriors who quit from exhaustion, swearing the black horse was a spirit, not a flesh-and-blood animal.

This summer he devised a plan to catch Night Wind without human help. He would be assisted by Snow, another of his fine horses, and his dog, Stranger, so named because as a pup he had wandered alone into camp. Talks to Horses nursed the sick, half-starved animal back to health. He grew to be a large, handsome, wolf-like animal with great strength and courage. He was fiercely loyal to his master and had saved Talks to Horses' life more than once during his explorations. Also, as a watchdog he was without equal. If Talks to Horses was planning to be away from camp for several hours, or even overnight, he would instruct Stranger to guard the extra horses and equipment, and Stranger would scare or chase interlopers away.

It had taken several weeks to prepare Stranger and Snow for this day. For his plan to work, Talks to Horses had to teach his animals to work together. He prepared a leather harness for Stranger, and to this he attached a halter to lead Snow. First, he held the rope and walked behind Stranger as they led the pony around the village. Then, he merely walked beside the two animals and increased the distances of their hikes. Next, he walked in front of the animals so Stranger was clearly leading Snow. After two weeks of this he rode a pony, and Stranger followed with Snow. At night he required them to stay to themselves away from the herds so Snow would develop a dependence on Stranger, his only nonhuman friend. Once the two animals were working well together, he trained Stranger to stay alone with Snow out on the plains, awaiting their master's call. When Talks to Horses whistled, they would come.

Right now they were stationed just below the hill on which Talks to Horses stood. Stranger would keep Snow there and protect him from predators. The main problem was whether the herd would circle back near this spot. He fingered the whistle hanging from a rawhide string around his neck. He had made it from a section of cane that grew only near the Talking Water River, five miles downstream from the Antelope village. Stranger could hear it from more than a mile away.

His heart accelerated as he watched Night Wind drink deeply. The horse's sides were beginning to bulge. Talks to Horses had followed this herd three days, and now was the first time the horse had drunk so much. Talks to Horses attributed the indulgence to the excessive heat and the blasting wind. The water would be cool and irresistibly refreshing. It was the custom of mustangs to graze up to ten miles away from their watering holes and then, when ready to drink, to gallop in for a long drink. The heat combined with the exercise made them thirstier than ever.

Talks to Horses leaned over and spoke softly to Honey, "When I say go, we will race after the herd. You must run with all your heart. We want to tire the black horse." Whether he understood the words or not, Honey tensed his muscles.

He eased the horse down the hill as the mustangs began to walk away from the water. Talks to Horses had not gone far when Night Wind sensed his presence and turned for the open range. He cried, "Go!" His horse lunged forward and soon was gaining on the water-logged herd.

The herd's path was as Talks to Horses had predicted from observing it over the past three days and from having chased it on two previous occasions. It was not going nearly so fast this time, however, and Night Wind was running about the speed of an ordinary horse that was not water-logged. At least he was until Talks to Horses began to draw near; then the black summoned extra energy and took off like a horse in a race.

Talks to Horses was not discouraged. Even as good as the black horse was, the water would sooner or later take its toll. He leaned forward and urged Honey on. Both were enjoying the chase after three days of anticipation and relative inactivity. Clad in nothing but a breech-cloth and a square of buffalo hide on his back for a sunshade, he felt refreshed—invigorated by the wind that dried the sweat on his lean, muscular body and lifted the two damp braids from his shoulders.

For Talks to Horses this kind of chase was far more exciting than chasing other men with an intent to kill. In this chase, which would end in friendship, he felt at one with Mother Earth. Every sense was stimulated more intensely than he could remember. The blue sky, the green grass and scattered oaks, the yellow wild flowers—all blended into a deeply satisfying picture of which he was an integral part. And he smelled every sweet scent and heard every melodious sound, despite the rumbling of the hoof beats. Nothing escaped his awareness, and everything was exciting. He was stirred by the muscles of the fine honey-colored horse that were extensions of his own muscles. Hot blood surged through their bodies as they stretched for more speed. The pounding of the horse's hoofs on the hot-baked soil made him feel as though Mother Earth were pushing him forward in this noble enterprise.

After completing the first circle of about twenty miles, most of the herd slowed perceptibly, but not Night Wind. He was going as fast as ever. Honey had not lost any of his speed either, though his breathing was harder. This gave Talks to Horses some concern. He had expected Night Wind to show signs of weakening by now, and he would call for Snow. He had to wonder if the strange mustang would ever tire. Maybe even when full of water he could run any two horses into the ground.

Talks to Horses leaned forward. "I had meant to rest you now, my pony, but you must run awhile longer. The black one has the strength of a river."

Before the second circle was completed, the herd had fallen back, leaving the race to Night Wind and Honey, but Honey was laboring hard to keep the pace. In fact, Talks to Horses was afraid the animal would die from his efforts. "Be strong," he admonished. "Only a little farther now." He felt the horse's pain and wished he could stop for a rest. It was impossible. To give up now was to lose the black horse forever.

Finally, he could see the hill in the distance, and he gave the whistle a long urgent blast. In moments Stranger emerged from behind the hill with Snow at his heels. Talks to Horses whistled again, and the two animals raced toward him. Snow drew alongside, and Talks to Horses, crouching on Honey, jumped to the fresh pony. He yelled, "Stay!" Stranger dropped back to protect Honey, whose lathered sides were heaving in and out as he struggled to breathe.

Talks to Horses was proud of his dog. He knew that despite the animal's longing to join the chase, his loyalty to his master overruled his personal preferences. Talks to Horses was moved by the generosity of Mother Earth, who provided man with sensuous beauty in the vegetable world and love and friendship in the animal world. As power surged through Snow's body and, in turn, Talks to Horses', he was also grateful to Father Sun for infusing them with this strength they needed.

Snow took longer to catch the black horse than Talks to Horses thought he would. Snow was a magnificent Spanish horse, the fastest in the Antelope band. As Snow labored, Talks to Horses knew he could never catch Night Wind in an even race. The thought made his anticipation even greater.

After a short while Night Wind slowed noticeably. Talks to Horses was beginning to fear the black horse would kill himself before admitting defeat. He pounded his knees against Snow, who responded with an extra surge of speed and drew near Night Wind. Talks to Horses swung his lasso over his head and flung the loop at the big mustang.

Night Wind fought furiously at the lasso about his neck and would have yanked Talks to Horses from Honey and dragged him across the plains if he had not been so exhausted from the chase. He seemed to realize that the more he struggled the tighter the lasso would become, though Talks to Horses was careful not to let it become so tight the pony choked. He despised the technique of choking a wild mustang down.

Others would keep the rope so tight the horse could not breathe but wheezed and squealed pitifully. Then they would throw the mustang to the ground, tie its legs, and loosen the lasso, moving it to the horse's mouth. Next they would let the pony up, filled with panic and covered with foam, to run and be thrown again and again until he gave up, often his spirit broken. At some point during the process they would breathe into the pony's nose. This last technique was the only part of the process Talks to Horses approved of.

When Night Wind finally realized he was not going to pull loose, he stood still and looked at Talks to Horses, who during the whole process thus far, had been calling with words of reassurance. Now he dismounted about twenty feet from Night Wind, making sure the mustang could see every movement he made.

"Don't be afraid, brave pony," he called soothingly, holding the lasso firmly in his right hand and extending his left. "You and I will be great friends."

Talks to Horses knew the horse, like all others, would want to hear, feel, and smell what had brought fear and pain into his world. Then he could begin the process of resignation. Right now, however, his fear, combined with exhaustion, outweighed his curiosity as he stood with his head sticking up, pulling against the rope. Talks to Horses continued to talk reassuringly and lovingly. He did not expect the mustang to understand his words, but he believed he could communicate with all animals with his heart. It was a gift Mother Earth gave all men. They had only to use and develop the gift.

After a while Night Wind stopped pulling at the rope and lowered his head in curiosity. Talks to Horses walked slowly forward, keeping his hand extended and the rope taut. The wild look had disappeared from the animal's eyes.

Talks to Horses touched his nose, "I am Talks to Horses, swift black pony, and I will call you Night Wind." He worked his hand slowly up the pony's flared nostrils, over his ears, and along his lathered neck. As he loosened the lasso, he said, "We will be loving friends, and you will sire swift, brave ponies for me." He reached into a leather pouch at his waist and drew out a handful of honey crystals. Night Wind ate tentatively.

After perhaps an hour of stroking and talking, Talks to Horses led Night Wind by the rope, which he had made into a bridle, and mounted Snow. He would collect his other animals, and begin his return trip. In three days he would ride triumphantly back into the Antelope village. All the people would crowd around to see this magnificent mustang some had seen at a distance and all had heard about. With Night Wind he could trade for anything or any woman he wanted.

He looked back over his shoulder at the proud black mustang. This horse he would keep.

5

THE CHAMPION

Talks to Horses entered Eagle's tepee looking grim. Eagle invited him to sit beside a small fire and then prepared a pipe. After four solemn puffs Talks to Horses said, "Coyote Droppings has taken Morning Dove. Yesterday he hid near that big dead cottonwood tree where she and Moonflower go to bathe. And when she came out of the water, he grabbed her. Moonflower says Morning Dove fought him until she fainted."

Eagle knew Coyote Droppings had wanted Morning Dove for his wife and had made no secret of his anger when Broken Foot gave her to Talks to Horses the year before. Knowing the kind of man Coyote Droppings was, Eagle expected trouble sooner or later. He searched Talks to Horses' eyes. "Has Coyote Droppings offered compensation?"

"Talks to Horses yesterday demanded Morning Dove's return. Coyote Droppings offered to kill him." His eyes dropped.

Eagle sat silently in contemplation. Although his brother was older by seven winters, Eagle was physically superior and was already a warrior of far greater renown. Talks to Horses would never be an outstanding warrior, but Eagle knew he was not a coward. He had seen his brother fight bravely at times, though killing men was distasteful to him. His passion was animals, and he spent most of his time exploring in the wilderness or working with the family herd, which, since Eagle had come into his own as a warrior, numbered over five hundred.

Talks to Horses was a favorite of the Antelope band. He had helped almost every warrior either by assisting with training his horse or by healing the animal's injury or illness. His medicine with animals was unsurpassed. Warriors even came from other Comanche bands to trade for his horses or benefit from his medicine.

Eagle laid his pipe aside. "Will Talks to Horses fight for his woman?"

"Eagle knows the kind of warrior Coyote Droppings is. He would kill me easily and with joy. Talks to Horses would be like a deer with a mountain lion."

Eagle nodded. "Talks to Horses has spoken truly." He had been to war with Coyote Droppings several times and knew him well. He was both fearless and vicious with his enemies. Eagle had seen him throw babies into the air and catch them on his lance during raids on enemy tribes. He was also cruel with his wives, often beating them mercilessly for minor offenses. He had killed his first one.

"Talks to Horses does not fear death, but his death at the hand of Coyote Droppings would be meaningless. Morning Dove would still be in his tepee."

"Has Talks to Horses talked to our father?" asked Eagle.

"Yesterday at sunset. He said Coyote Droppings would kill me, and it would be a great loss for him and for our band. He said Eagle should represent his brother." He looked at Eagle with a mixture of hope and pain that he had to ask so great a favor from his younger brother.

Eagle looked into the fire without expression. He knew tribal law permitted a wronged person to seek a champion, and he was proud that Long Lance and Talks to Horses had shown such confidence in him. Also, he despised Coyote Droppings. Killing him would serve two purposes. It would rid Talks to Horses of his problem, and it would enhance Eagle's reputation.

He had suspected for some time he would have to confront the villainous warrior. When Coyote Droppings heard talk that Eagle would soon be a war chief, he was infuriated. It was a position he desperately desired but would never achieve because of his wicked disposition and his stupidity. He was incapable of planning and leading a successful attack, and he was getting more and more jealous of those who could, especially of those younger than he. Eagle had seen the resentment and jealousy in his eyes. The man was not to be trusted when one's back was turned.

"Shall Eagle ask for compensation?"

"Bring Morning Dove back to my tepee! She hates Coyote Droppings. Last night she tried to kill him while he was asleep, but he woke up and beat her."

Eagle nodded. Morning Dove was both courageous and beautiful. She was also affectionate, intelligent, and skilled at cooking, tanning, sewing, and other women's work. As was the custom among the Comanches, a warrior might share his wife with his brother. Talks to Horses had sent Morning Dove to his tepee on two occasions when Eagle was depressed from losing friends on raids.

These experiences, along with numerous meals shared in Talks to Horses' tepee, had helped them form a close friendship. He did not covet her for his own wife; but when he was ready to take a wife, he would like to find someone like her. Right now he was too much concerned with becoming a great warrior.

He looked at Talks to Horses and said tentatively, "Coyote Droppings has those two big white horses he took in the raid below the Stinking Buffalo River. Except for your black mustang, they are the most beautiful of horses, especially the stallion. Eagle could ask for them. They are wasted on Coyote Droppings."

Talks to Horses' eyes lit up. "What animals! Our father says they come from a far-off land of white men where there are many such horses." He shook his head. "It is useless to talk about them. He would not give them to Broken Foot in exchange for Morning Dove. He will not give them to Talks to Horses." He pounded his fists on the ground for emphasis. "What a war horse that white stallion could be."

"The mare is almost ready to foal. Coyote Droppings could have that."

The light faded from Talks to Horses' eyes as he thought about the possibility of a trade. "It is unpleasant to think of Morning Dove remaining in his tepee."

The two brothers sat in silence for a long time, until Eagle said, "In the morning Eagle will go to Coyote Droppings' tepee." After they quietly shared another pipeful of tobacco, Talks to Horses left with a lighter heart.

At first light, Eagle rose and sat prayerfully facing the east. The bright rays of the winter sun warmed his half-naked body and infused his spirit with strength and resolution. He felt the Great Spirit was giving him strong medicine. For more than an hour he sat in silent communion, until the sun moved behind a dark cloud. Since the buck was his source of power, he put on his buckskin pants and shirt, and he strapped on his knife with the metal blade and the handle carved from an antler.

He found Coyote Droppings and Morning Dove outside the abductor's tepee. One end of a six-foot rope was tied around her feet; the other was tied to an elm tree. She was working on some buffalo hides, which would soon be ready for trading, and he was sitting with a buffalo robe draped over his broad shoulders watching her possessively. He was proud of his new trophy and wanted the whole band to see him with her. She had a large bruise below her left eye, and she moved stiffly. Her eyes filled with hope when Eagle approached. Coyote Droppings' small eyes showed annoyance, and his thick lips moved soundlessly, trying to frame appropriate words.

"Talks to Horses wants his wife back," announced Eagle.

"Let Talks to Horses come and get her," Coyote Droppings snorted derisively.

"Eagle has come for her."

Coyote Droppings was unprepared for what he was facing, and it took him several minutes to think of something to say. Eagle could see it had not occurred to him that Talks to Horses was the son of Long Lance and there might be serious repercussions from taking the wife of the great chief's son. Once before, he had crossed Long Lance, and the chief had thrust a lance through his left arm. Coyote Droppings massaged his arm unconsciously. He knew he had been fortunate that Long Lance had not killed him. Eagle was sure he would be trying to figure out what Long Lance would do if he killed Eagle.

"Talks to Horses gave Broken Foot ten horses for Morning Dove. Coyote will send Talks to Horses five horses and a fine buffalo robe." He would never acknowledge the degrading name assigned him by the other Antelope warriors.

"Two horses will be enough."

"Two?" Coyote Droppings asked suspiciously.

"The two white ones."

Coyote Droppings laughed loudly without mirth. "Those two horses are worth a hundred wives. The stallion is the swiftest and smartest horse in the world, and the mare is almost as good. Besides she will soon foal."

"Talks to Horses will give Coyote Droppings the colt." Eagle emphasized the last part of his name.

"Coyote will never give those horses to Talks to Horses." He spat on the ground in front of Eagle. "Or anyone else."

"Then Eagle will take Morning Dove back." He moved toward her with his hand outstretched, and she eagerly rose to join him.

"No!" Throwing off his buffalo robe, Coyote Droppings jumped to his feet looking furious. He was half a head shorter than Eagle but broader, with large bulging muscles. He flexed his shoulders and chest to intimidate the younger warrior.

Eagle looked evenly into Coyote Droppings' eyes, unmoved by the other's fury or his body. "Does Coyote Droppings wish to make another offer?"

The anger in Coyote Droppings' eyes was mixed with confusion. Eagle knew this stupid man expected him to back down at his show of strength and formidable anger. What Eagle showed him was a tall, strong, confident warrior ready for combat if necessary. He knew Coyote Droppings had never fought unless he was certain of victory. Now he had to face a warrior who might be his better. Coyote Droppings had observed Eagle in battle and knew him for a superb fighter.

Seeing a crowd of women and children beginning to form and not wanting it to swell further, Coyote Droppings smiled with condescension. "Tell Talks to Horses he will get twelve horses, two more than he gave Broken Foot." He swelled his chest as he looked out over his audience. "Coyote is always fair."

Eagle snorted his disgust. "Except for the whites, Coyote Droppings' whole herd of diseased animals is not worth three of the ponies Talks to Horses gave Broken Foot."

Several warriors who had joined the crowd laughed loudly at Eagle's remark. Coyote Droppings looked with a hint of panic in his eyes. The crowd was swelling rapidly. In his dense mind he would be weighing the pleasure of owning the white horses against his pride in possessing Morning Dove, who so far had brought him no pleasure.

Knowing how much Coyote Droppings liked to show off the horses, Eagle was sure he would gladly return Morning Dove if he could do so without loss of face, something that was now no longer possible. It was as Eagle had planned.

Coyote Droppings puffed out his barrel chest. "Tell Talks to Horses that twelve horses is Coyote's last offer, but not the white ones."

Eagle had come expecting to fight. In the night he had a dream in which Coyote Droppings shot him in the back during a war with the Apache. The best thing to do was exterminate him now; the band would be better off without such disgusting people. He disregarded Coyote Droppings' offer and, extending his left hand, he drew his knife with the other and said to Morning Dove. "Come, it is time to return to the tepee of Talks to Horses." A cloud partially obscured the sun.

The kidnapper jumped between them with his knife drawn and ready. Eagle slipped off his shirt. "Eagle is surprised Coyote Droppings did not wait until his back was turned, killer of women."

At that taunt, Coyote Droppings lunged at Eagle, who jumped aside and at the same time slashed Coyote Droppings across the chest. If the blade had not struck a rib, the fight would already be over. Coyote Droppings looked down at the blood and was infuriated. He squared off again, retreating a step or two. Eagle followed cautiously. Too late he realized Coyote Droppings had maneuvered to the front of his tepee, where his lance was propped near the opening. Coyote Droppings grabbed it and replaced his knife in its sheath. Indicating his chest with a dip of his head, Coyote Droppings said wickedly, "For that you die." He did not lunge this time. He moved slowly like a cat .

Now it was Eagle's turn to retreat. He rotated backward until he was in the great circle in the middle of the village. This was where the great dances were held, and it was where Coyote Droppings wanted him to be. He wanted the whole band to see him kill Eagle. Eagle wished for his own lance and told himself never to expect someone like Coyote Droppings to fight fairly. Disadvantaged as he was, however, he did not lose his confidence. He believed his supe-

The Champion

rior quickness and intelligence would make the lance ineffective.

Coyote Droppings was pleased to see the large crowd gathering. His movements were exaggerated in an effort to give grandeur to his conquest. He made numerous playful stabs at Eagle, who jumped aside. Coyote Droppings' expression was one of wicked pleasure. He was enjoying his anticipated victory. He would gain much glory from killing the son of Long Lance. He would make a sport of it; and when all had beheld his greatness, he would kill his victim.

Eagle was careful not to underestimate Coyote Dropping's ability with the lance. It was his favorite weapon, and Eagle had seen him kill three Utes in personal combat with it. In time, Eagle began to breathe hard and slow his evasive jumps perceptibly, in hopes Coyote Droppings would be too stupid and too overconfident to suspect a trick.

It was not long before his apparent fatigue made Coyote Droppings more reckless; and to add to the effect, Eagle let the lance point brush his arm. He grabbed the wound quickly and leaned sideways, giving the appearance it was deep and painful. Blood seeped through his fingers as he squeezed the wound. At the sight of a tired and wounded prey, Coyote Droppings shouted a war cry and lunged again at Eagle, this time expecting the point to plunge into his chest.

Once more Eagle jumped aside, this time with lightning quickness, and made a catlike step forward. Pivoting, he grabbed the extended lance with both hands. Coyote Droppings stumbled slightly with surprise, at which time Eagle, holding the lance firmly, fell on his back, pulling the big warrior toward him. With his feet he pushed Coyote Droppings into the air and over his head. Coyote Droppings landed on his back with a loud "Ugh!"

Eagle sprang to his feet holding the lance, its point toward Coyote Droppings. As the other warrior struggled to his feet gasping for breath, Eagle could have lanced him, but a quick execution would no longer satisfy him. He wanted to punish Coyote Droppings, who stood before him like a cornered animal. Eagle looked at him contemptuously. The villain was squared off, his knife ready. He threw the lance far over Coyote Droppings' head and out of sight. "Eagle gives you a chance to take to your tepee, since you must fight knife with knife."

Coyote Droppings eyed Eagle warily. He had seen the younger warrior's quickness and knew he could not win with knives. Grandly, he threw his knife toward his tepee and beckoned Eagle toward him with both hands outstretched. "Coyote gives you the edge, little boy."

Eagle had underestimated his opponent. He had not realized a man could be both stupid and clever. If Eagle killed Coyote Droppings with a knife, he would enjoy no real victory. Some would doubt his medicine because he had refused to fight a despised warrior on equal terms. If Eagle threw away the knife, he might lose the fight and suffer shame, if not death. Coyote Droppings was one of the strongest men among the Antelopes, while Eagle knew he had not yet reached his own full strength. He had been foolish to throw away the lance. The other warriors would have approved Coyote Droppings' death on the lance, because he had introduced the weapon.

"Is Eagle afraid?" called Coyote Droppings.

"Eagle fears neither man nor Coyote Droppings." He tossed his knife out of the circle. As he did so, he saw Long Lance nod to him confidently. He felt an extra measure of strength.

At the insult Coyote Droppings rushed Eagle with his head down like a charging bull. Eagle stepped aside and gave Coyote Droppings a powerful chop with both hands made into a big fist. The blow slammed into the small of his enemy's back. The crowd cheered at the great "Oof!" from Coyote Droppings' tortured lungs. The cheers excited Eagle.

Coyote Droppings turned and straightened slowly, obviously in pain. Quickly Eagle grabbed his neck in a hammerlock. It was like grabbing a buffalo bull. Coyote Droppings struggled fiercely. Taking advantage of his lower center of gravity, he clasped Eagle's legs and lifted him in the air; then he lunged sideways, landing on top of him. Eagle was shocked at how much heavier Coyote Droppings was than he had estimated, and his upper body strength was not to be believed.

Perched on Eagle's chest, Coyote Droppings gripped his neck with vice-like hands, digging his thumbs into the windpipe. For the first time in his life, Eagle was close to panic. This was worse than when he faced the white buffalo, because he, like all Comanches, believed the spirit of a strangled warrior could not enter the Great Spirit's hunting grounds.

Just as Coyote Droppings' short legs had been an advantage to him, Eagle put his longer legs to good use. Calling on his last breath and strength, he rolled backward and brought his legs up around Coyote Droppings' head. Then he jerked the villain backward and crashed his head into the cold, hard ground. It sounded like a crushed melon.

As the crowd cheered, Eagle rose unsteadily to his feet and placed his right knee in the upper back of his dazed opponent. "Now you die, killer of women!" With both hands under Coyote Droppings' chin, he yanked backward with a twisting motion. The neck bone snapped loudly.

With one foot on the dead man, Eagle stood to accept the thunderous cheers. He looked through the crowd to see Morning Dove standing beside Talks to Horses; both were smiling and waving their arms enthusiastically. Long Lance came to Eagle's side and proudly draped a buffalo robe over his son's blood-smeared body.

The champion would spend the rest of the winter afternoon in his tepee thanking the Great Spirit for giving him strong medicine. Then a grateful Morning Dove would come to him with his favorite food. She would cleanse his aching body and doctor his wounds. After sharing her companionship through the night, he would rise up with the sun and claim the white horses.

Warlords of the West

6

THE CHASE

Moonflower let the horse have his head as they galloped through the bluebonnets that almost obliterated the trail. Even though her father, Broken Foot, had warned her against riding out so far alone, she felt nothing could go wrong on a day like this one. Everything about it was exhilarating. She inhaled the air, heavy with the scent of spring. She had never felt happier or more secure. She leaned over and patted Flame, a gift from her father at the death of her mother. Now, one winter had passed, and the horse was almost a part of her. She had worked with him daily. She felt she could almost command him with her thoughts.

Flame was finer than any horse she had seen, solid black except for a flame of white on his face. She reflected with pleasure on her father's compliments about the obedience of the horse. Broken Foot was, in his day, as good as any rider in the Antelope band, and he had predicted she would have much difficulty training such a highly spirited stallion, even if she had him gelded. He suggested she get one of the warriors to tame the horse.

Talks to Horses was the only warrior she would trust Flame with, because she hated the cruel methods used by others; but he was away on one of his explorations. However, she had studied his techniques of taming horses, and she used them successfully with Flame. As she had hoped, there developed a mutual respect and devotion between her and the horse.

She was startled from her reverie by a warrior who stepped out from a small clump of trees just off the trail ahead. Wearing only a breech-cloth and moccasins with leggings, he was a tall, muscular man, handsome even in his vermillion and yellow war paint. She recognized him at once, and her heart beat faster. He was Eagle, the son of the great war chief, Long Lance. She had secretly admired Eagle for over a year now.

"You're far from home, Little One," he said as she rode up.

"Moonflower is not lost, and she is not little," she said defensively, holding her back erect and looking grown up. "She has seen fifteen winters."

Eagle looked at her with new interest, noting her well-shaped legs. She had pulled her doeskin skirt well above her knees so she could sit astride her pony as a man would. Eagle nodded, "Soon Moonflower will be a grown Antelope. Unless the Ute catches her. He has a hunting party coming this way. She is fortunate Eagle's warriors saw him first, or she would be in his camp tonight."

"Moonflower will turn back!" She was horrified by an image of herself as a captive. She knew the Ute would probably torture her awhile and then make a slave of her.

"No. The advance scout, who has already passed this way, will see your trail end here. He may think he has been seen and return to warn the others. Then our efforts would be like those of the coyote that waits in vain for the prairie dog to come from an empty hole."

She looked around and did not see anyone else.

"There are ten of us hidden. Five are with the horses behind that little hill over there."

"What is Moonflower to do?"

"Can you find your way home from the Lake of the Sun?" He pointed south toward the lake.

"Yes." She had been there only once and was uncertain, but she did not want Eagle to know that.

"Ride straight to that tallest tree. A trail is nearby. Follow the trail to the lake." He must have seen uncertainty in her face. He added. "If you are not sure, wait by the tree, and Eagle will come for you later."

"Moonflower can find the way," she said proudly. She nudged the sides of Flame and spoke urgent words in his ears. The horse responded with a burst of speed. After a few minutes of hard riding she looked back and saw no traces of the young warrior. Her confidence flagged. She wished Eagle could ride home with her.

Flame's hoofs pounded in an exciting rhythm, almost like that of the war drums, she thought. She was stirred passionately and wished she could ride like this forever. She loved the feeling of superior speed and power she shared with the horse, and she savored the bite of the fragrant wind whipping through her clothing and blowing her hair wildly. She had experienced a brief encounter with danger and had been saved by a handsome warrior. Now she was riding the world's fastest and most beautiful horse toward a lovely lake, where she would enjoy wading in the water and perhaps bask awhile in the sun before going home. It occurred to her there had not been many thrilling moments like this in her life. For warriors like Eagle they were commonplace.

When she reached the woods, she stopped to look for the tree Eagle had pointed to. She had taken her eyes from it, and now she could not identify it. Most of the trees looked alike up close. She looked around for familiar landmarks. There were none. If she had ever come this far, she could not remember it. Stretching to the eastern horizon was rolling grassland, dotted with oak trees and patches of bluebonnets. Here and there were low, rugged hills covered with cedars. The landscape to her right towards home looked about the same.

After searching only a few minutes, she found a faintly worn path near what could have been Eagle's "tallest tree." It seemed a little taller than the others. She dismounted. Flame was sweating and breathing heavily; a walk through the woods would refresh them both. She stroked the horse's neck and spoke words of praise. She promised him delicious grazing and fresh, clear water when they arrived at the lake.

Leading Flame, she walked into the woods. Her exhilaration had worn off, and she was feeling anxious. She half wished she had waited by the tree. Even now she could turn back, but she did not want Eagle to think she could not take care of herself. She stepped forward with a renewed confidence that did not last long. Though she had been alone in an unfamiliar woods before, she was always within shouting distance of companions. Being a Comanche girl, she had not been taught the ways of the woods. Perhaps even now she was walking in circles, as she had heard lost people sometimes do. Flame was her comfort. She remembered seeing ponies that had found their way back to the village after being abandoned in battle. Certainly, Flame could take them back home if she could not.

The woods were moist and scented by trees and wildflowers. It was a comfortable environment in deep contrast with the violent world of the warriors. Moonflower found herself smiling and humming a nature song. Soon, she began to feel one with the woods, as though she were an animal meant never to leave this, her natural habitat. Although her feet were protected by nothing but soft moccasins, and the sticks and rocks on the ground bruised her feet, she was oblivious to the pain. Her spirit was one with Mother Earth.

In this state she did not notice the increased nervousness of Flame, the flaring of his nostrils and the shaking of his head. When finally the pony snorted loudly, Moonflower grew alert. Her heart raced when she heard a low growl. She hurried her pace, hoping to leave the sound behind. The growl grew louder. She wished she could mount Flame and gallop away, but the undergrowth was too heavy. Limbs and brush were so thick the horse had barely enough room to move along the trail, even without a rider.

The bear broke from the brush just behind them and roared like thunder. Flame sprang forward, knocking Moonflower aside, and plunged along the path out of sight. She regained her balance and looked back. The big, ugly grizzly was only a dozen feet away. He was standing on his hind legs roaring, his long yellow teeth bared. If it were not for the heavy brush, he would already have her. A slender athletic girl, Moonflower was a good, strong runner; and she did not hesitate now, despite a weakness in her knees.

Her smaller size was an advantage as she raced through the woods. Limbs lashed at her face and tore her soft doeskin blouse and skirt apart. Though she had spent hours decorating them, she could not take the time to worry about them. The condition of her feet bothered her most. They were moist from wounds made by the rubble on the ground.

Her pain and fright were in extreme contrast with the exhilaration of the ride to the woods, yet there was an excitement that gave her strength and a clear head. In the back of her mind was the thought that none of the other women had experienced such a chase. They knew cooking, tanning hides, and caring for babies. Occasionally, some of them accompanied their husbands on raids and hunts, but they did not take part in the action. None she knew had been involved in a chase that had death as the price for losing. She could hardly wait to get back to the village to tell her sister, Morning Dove, of her adventure. If she got back.

Moonflower knew now why her father had frequently cautioned her against going out alone. The warriors who went out alone had knives, bows, and lances; and they knew the ways of animals. She knew very little about bears, and her only weapon was a small knife tied to her waist. It was useless against so mighty an enemy as this bear. Her only real defense was flight, and she knew her stamina could not match the bear's.

When she burst into the clearing, she was thirty-five or forty feet from the lake. Not seeing Flame, she ran to the edge of the water; the bear was not far behind. Excitement surged when she saw Flame about three hundred feet down the lake. She fought back an impulse to run after the horse. The bear would surely catch her before she reached him. She stood looking at the water as the bear crashed from the woods with angry growls. She looked down into the water, a straight drop of fifteen feet. Hoping the bear would not jump after her, she yanked off her dilapidated skirt, and dived.

The water was cold, taking her breath away; even so, she stayed under a few seconds to put some distance between herself and the shore. The water was clear enough to see perch swimming near. She pushed her way back toward the surface and shook water from her eyes. Treading water, she slipped off the doeskin blouse, which was soaked and dragging her down.

Feeling light and stronger now, she looked up at the bear, which was still at the edge of the bank looking down at her and roaring with disappointment. She hoped he would give up and go away.

Still treading water, she looked around and tried to think what to do. It was a good half mile across the lake, not a difficult swim if she were fresh. Having grown up near rivers, she had swum farther than that before. She knew she would not be able to make it now, though. The desperate run through the woods had left her fatigued. Her breath was coming in gasps. She looked around again, trying not to panic. There was not even a floating limb to cling to. She saw herself as the little white-tailed rabbit in her brother's snare. Did the rabbit understand death was near? she wondered.

She turned and swam frantically with heavy arms toward Flame, her only source of help. He had already run from the bear; she was afraid he would run again. Self-preservation had overcome any sense of loyalty the horse had developed. Her disappointment brought tears to her eyes.

She knew she must discipline herself, because she would die of exhaustion at this frantic pace. At dance fires she had heard many tales of strength and valor. She remembered one Eagle had told. He was nearly defeated by a great white buffalo, but he never gave up despite tremendous pain. Determination surged within. She would survive!

To catch her breath, she floated on her back a few minutes. Remembering her earlier feeling of union with Mother Earth, she sought renewed strength from the water and the sun. "Father Sun, give Moonflower strength," she prayed. Shortly, she began to feel stronger and calmer. The important thing was to avoid despair and to use her resources wisely. Also, she must let Flame know in some way what he must do. She wondered if he could understand her thoughts.

Turning her head slightly, she saw the bear had followed along the shore and was waiting. While she rested, the slight current had carried her perhaps a hundred and fifty feet, and the bank was not nearly so steep where the bear stood. He was looking over the edge with interest, as though he were evaluating the possibility of a jump.

Moonflower knew this bear must be the one the hunters called Old Destroyer. He did not behave as other bears but had a fierceness and determination that made even the best hunters avoid him unless in a hunting party. She had heard most bears would not bother a man unless provoked. This bear was said to have ambushed hunters and even tracked them back to their villages where he made night raids, especially if the hunters had wounded him.

"Come, Flame!" She tried to make her voice firm and reassuring. She even swam another hundred feet. The horse was not running. He was tossing his head and eyeing the bear, which was showing little interest in anything but the trapped swimmer. Moonflower was encouraged; perhaps the horse would not run this time. Horses are good swimmers, she thought; perhaps Flame would jump into the water and save her. Then she remembered Flame had never been in water. Perhaps he was as afraid of it as of the bear. "Come, Flame!"

Flame looked at Moonflower and ran to the edge of the lake where he was only sixty or seventy feet from the bear. There, the shore sloped gently into the water. The bear turned his head toward Flame and roared. The horse backed away from the edge of the water. Encouraged by Flame's initial movements forward, Moonflower had been swimming toward him. Seeing him back away brought renewed panic and exhaustion. Her arms and shoulders burned with pain, and the air rattled in her throat and lungs. "Flame!" she gasped as she saw the bear walk down to the water and step in.

Flame ran a few paces toward the water and snorted. The bear turned angrily back to frighten him away. Moonflower's vision blurred slightly; she could not swim any farther. She sank, her legs searching for the bottom of the lake. It had to be only a few feet below. Not finding it, her weary legs somehow propelled her back to the surface. Unable to touch bottom and unable to swim any farther, she could only thrash at the water with lifeless arms.

She was oblivious to everything but survival, and that was becoming less important. She thought it might be a pleasant release to sink and breathe the lovely clear water. She sank. This time the bottom was where it should be. A good forward push and she could stand with her head just out of the water. When she cleared her eyes, she expected to see the bear in front of her, waiting.

He was not in the water. He was standing fifty feet away fighting with Flame. Moonflower's heart again filled with pride, and she forgot her exhaustion. Her only thought was to get out of the water and help her horse. Flame was rearing up and kicking at the bear with his front hoofs. The bear was slashing back with his long iron-like claws—an uneven match. Blood flowed from Flame's right shoulder. He backed away and the bear followed, excited by the blood of a new prey.

Terrified for her horse, Moonflower felt a new surge of energy. She swam a few more strokes until her knees bumped the bottom; then she trudged through the mud and up onto the shore. She wanted to run to Flame's aid, but she thought better of it; she was naked and without a weapon, not even a stick. Instead, she ran and stumbled along the bank until she was about a hundred feet from the fray. "Come, Flame!" she shouted with more strength than she thought she had. Her voice reverberated along the far side of the lake.

Flame had reared up again and was pawing ineffectually at the bear. On hearing Moonflower's voice, the horse dropped to all fours and raced to his mistress, the bear right behind. Enraged at losing his prey, the bear moved fast, and Moonflower had to be ready. As the pony came near, she grabbed his mane with both hands and swung herself on his back as she had done often in play.

The bear roared as Moonflower and Flame raced along the bank, leaving him far behind. For Moonflower the exhilaration had returned as the late air nipped her wet body, and her heart reverberated to the pounding of the horses's hoofs on the rocky shore.

When she began to get over the thrill of escape, she looked around for a trail out of the woods that surrounded the lake. She thought there would be one at the west end. She wondered if she had missed it while she was riding away from the bear. Did she dare turn around and go back for a better look? she wondered. She decided not to. She

followed the trail that circled the lake all the way around to the other side. There was no trail out. It was getting dark, and she had to fight panic. Should she turn things over to Flame? She decided to ride back around the lake and look more carefully. Surely the bear would be gone by now.

The breeze blowing off the lake was getting cold. She had only her long hair lying on her breast to keep in her body heat. It did not help much. Fear gripped her as she rounded the west end of the lake again. Even if she found the trail now, she would have to ride through the woods in the dark.

A rider on a big white horse stood in the trail just ahead. He waved and galloped toward her. "Are you lost, Little One?" It was Eagle. He had on a buckskin shirt now.

She wanted to jump from her pony and throw herself into his arms. "A-attacked by a t-terrible bear and had to r-run." She could not stop her teeth from chattering.

"That is why Moonflower left this behind." He started toward her holding out her skirt.

"No!" she shouted in alarm, covering herself with her hands. "D-drop it and t-turn around. P-please!"

Eagle smiled and pulled off his shirt. He dropped it and the skirt onto the ground and turned his back to the pretty Antelope girl. "The trail at this end of the lake is hard to see because it comes out of the woods behind that giant oak tree." He pointed again. "Eagle was afraid Moonflower would miss it. He found her skirt by the trail up there." He pointed with his left hand. "Did the bear take it from her?" There was amusement in his tone.

She stepped into her skirt. "W-what about the U-Ute?"

"We lost him. We had not waited long when the advance scout came back alone. Smiling Dog shot him, and he screamed. The others were scared away." His voice was filled with disgust.

"Th-that was b-bad of Smiling D-Dog," she said as she pulled on Eagle's shirt. It was warm and full of comfort. She rolled up the sleeves and climbed onto Flame.

Eagle turned toward her again. "What about that bear?"

Moonflower said proudly. "It is a st-story that will take t-time to tell pr-properly."

Eagle grinned his disbelief and headed his pony toward the trail back. Moonflower followed, annoyed but happy. When others heard her story and saw the wounds on her and Flame, they would believe. She would be envied by all the other maidens and admired by the warriors. Eagle would have to believe her, too.

THE COURTING

PART 1:
THE SUGGESTION

Eagle sat across from his brother, Talks to Horses, in the latter's tepee. On Talks to Horses' left was his wife, Morning Dove, who had just served a dinner of fresh buffalo hump cooked the way Eagle liked it, red in the middle. Talks to Horses' son, Wild Horse, sat at his right. He was a handsome, muscular boy, the only child Morning Dove had borne her husband in their seven years of marriage. However, the bulge under her doeskin skirt indicated she would soon bear another.

After the two men and the boy had eaten hungrily, Talks to Horses prepared a pipeful of real tobacco. He had traded a white and grey paint to a warrior who had obtained a bag of the aromatic mixture in a raid on the Spaniard to the south. He took a long draw from the pipe and blew the smoke toward the top of the tepee. "Eagle needs a wife," he said as he handed the pipe to his brother.

Eagle pondered the statement. He had been feeling a deep loneliness all winter, and he had enjoyed the family feeling during his frequent visits to his brother's tepee. Occasionally, he thought it would be pleasant to have a wife like Morning Dove, and he derived pleasure from playing with his nephew. But he would have to make sacrifices. He shook his head. "Eagle is often gone on raids and hunts. When he is not away, he needs to be alone to make medicine. A woman would weaken his medicine."

Talks to Horses shook his head stubbornly. "Eagle has seen only twenty-five winters, yet he has been a war chief many moons. He is already one of the Antelope band's greatest chiefs. He does not have to prove himself any more."

Eagle puffed contemplatively and then blew the smoke upward. It was good tobacco. "Eagle is no longer concerned with proving himself as a warrior. He has promised the Great Spirit he will use his medicine to become a great leader of The People. One day his people will need him."

Talks to Horses had nothing to say to that as he took his turn with the pipe. As though relieved to have the problem resolved, he puffed hungrily. After a few moments of silence Morning Dove nudged him. He grunted and cleared his throat. "Our father is a great war chief. He had a wife when he was younger than Eagle. His medicine has always been strong." Eagle leaned slightly forward, interested.

Talks to Horses added, "Long Lance says a man's spirit lives on through his sons and their sons after them." He pointed the pipe at Eagle. "If Eagle died now, nothing of him would remain."

Eagle nodded his head in assent. "This is truth."

"A woman will help Eagle be even greater. She will take care of his tepee, his meals, his weapons—everything. Eagle will have even more time to make medicine." He handed the pipe to Eagle. "And there will be no more lonely nights. She will always be there."

Eagle sat silently for awhile thinking. He held the pipe without smoking it. Talks to Horses motioned for Morning Dove and Wild Horse to leave. Their faces showed disappointment, and they left reluctantly. When they were gone, Eagle said, "Eagle has thought of taking a wife, but it would be better not to marry than have a wife that is always a problem—like the wife of Takes a Chance. Eagle knows about horses and weapons, wars and hunts. How would he choose a wife?"

Talks to Horses spoke as though the thought had just occurred to him. "There is a woman who would be a good wife for you."

"Who is this woman?"

"Moonflower." Talks to Horses said her name dramatically.

Eagle's eyes tightened in a smile. So this was the purpose of the good dinner and fine tobacco. Morning Dove wanted Eagle to marry her little sister. She had helped raise her sister, and now she wanted to pick her husband. "Moonflower is a only a girl," scoffed Eagle.

"When did you last see her?"

He reflected a moment. "It has been many moons. When she was chased by the bear."

"Soon she will see her eighteenth winter. She is as graceful as the antelope, and she is tall and straight like a willow shoot. Also, she has a loving disposition and can work hard."

"You exaggerate. You have been coached to say pretty things."

Talks to Horses looked hurt. "It is all true. And Morning Dove has taught her all the things a wife should know." He folded his arms across his chest. "There is not another maiden like her anywhere."

Eagle was suspicious. "Why have you not married her?"

"Moonflower has a strong will. She does not want to be a second wife in her sister's tepee."

Eagle nodded. He liked spirit in women as well as in horses. "There must be many warriors seeking to marry this wonderful maiden."

"There are, but Moonflower will not have any of them, and she is Broken Foot's last child. Morning Dove thinks he will not make her marry someone she does not want."

"If the gifts were great?"

Talks to Horses was thoughtful. "Who can say? Broken Foot is getting old and has a great desire to increase the quality and size of his herd. He gave Morning Dove to Talks to Horses for ten fine horses, even though he had meant to give her to the son of Little River." Talks to Horses smiled. "He gave the son a fine black and white mustang that could run all day and not get tired. To Little River he gave a big sorrel. What a horse!"

As usual, when Talks to Horses started discussing horses, he lost interest in all other subjects. Eagle interrupted. "Would Moonflower be interested in me?"

"You saved her life once."

"That was many moons ago. She was not a woman then."

"Morning Dove says Moonflower has not forgotten. She says Moonflower also admires Eagle as the greatest of warriors." Talks to Horses put his hand on Eagle's shoulder. "It is only necessary to arrange a meeting. She is not one to slip into a warrior's tepee at night."

Eagle puffed at the pipe then held it out to Talks to Horses. "Her brother has just returned from an unsuccessful raid."

"And we have a bay stallion in our herd he admires. Offer it to him in return for his help," suggested Talks to Horses as he took the pipe.

Standing Buck was the last of Broken Foot's sons. He was a strong and daring fighter, but he had little wealth, since he had not ridden out many times. He had received no help from his older brothers, who had been killed in a raid against the Ute, and their herds had been killed at the funeral. Consequently, he was more than happy to accept the bay from Eagle and help him with his courtship. He told Eagle about Moonflower's habits and when he might encounter her privately, since a public meeting would be out of the question for Eagle.

Part 2:
THE MAIDEN

Moonflower still had Flame, the black horse Broken Foot had given her, and she loved to ride him along the river in the afternoons, despite the almost fatal encounter with the bear. Standing Buck told Eagle where and when he could expect her to begin the ride.

The Blue Water River was deep and wide near the Antelope village. The trees were dense, and there was plentiful wildlife. This stretch of the river was especially pretty in the early summer with thousands of white, yellow, and blue wildflowers adding variety to the deep green. Eagle arranged to be there when Moonflower began her ride the afternoon following his deal with Standing Buck.

She appeared. Eagle had a sense of unreality, as though she were riding out of some kind of dream. He had been thinking of her as she was before. Now the bud had blossomed into a lovely flower. She was wearing a plain doeskin blouse and skirt of the same material. It was pulled high so she could sit astride her horse.

Eagle wanted to wait and watch, but he rode toward her as though he were also out for a pleasant ride and just happened along at this time. Instead of moving Flame from the narow path so Eagle could ride by, Moonflower pulled up to wait.

This meeting was crucial in their relationship, and Eagle felt slightly nervous. According to Comanche custom, if she ignored him or was cool, he would be obligated to forget the project. He hoped that would not happen; he had already begun to think of her as his wife, and seeing her confirmed that she was the woman for his tepee.

Showing no surprise or shyness, Moonflower gave him a smile of recognition and welcome. The feeling Eagle had was not just relief. He felt a warmth and joy he had never known before. Though he had been with women occasionally in the evening—when they slipped in under his tepee— they seldom talked. He had hardly ever had a daylight social confrontation with an eligible maiden. Even that time when he helped Moonflower find her way home from the Lake of the Sun, they had ridden home silently in the dark.

She saw he was ill at ease and spoke first. Her manner was relaxed, and her voice was full of music. "The path is not wide enough for two ponies. What shall we do?"

The way she said *we* caused Eagle's heart to accelerate. She made him feel he held a special place in her life. He relaxed. "It is wide enough for two walking." He dismounted from his war horse, Whirlwind, and walked to meet her. Though she could easily slide down from her pony unaided, she waited for him to help her. The feel of her supple waist and the touch of her hands on his naked shoulders electrified him.

Unlike many other maidens Moonflower did not chatter away about nothing. Instead she walked quietly by Eagle's side waiting for him to speak. When he did, he spoke with ease, his voice deep and resonant. "Eagle had forgotten the river could be so pretty. It seems only a little while ago he bathed in a river like this on a cold fall morning."

"Why did Eagle do that?"

"For purification—before receiving a vision."

"Please tell Moonflower about being a warrior."

As they walked along the water's edge, he told her stories of raids and wars. She was enthralled and amazed he could have done so many great and exciting things in so short a career. When he mentioned the fight with Coyote Droppings, she said, "I saw that. It is the most exciting thing I have ever seen. Broken Foot praised Eagle's conduct and said some day he would be a great man and lead The People."

He smiled, pleased. "I have talked too long. Moonflower should talk." Their shoulders brushed as they walked.

"You have already heard my most exciting adventure. With Old Destroyer."

"That was long ago. Tell it again." He wanted to hear the soft melodies of her voice.

Moonflower began with Broken Foot's present of Flame and how she trained him. Then she told of her feelings on seeing Eagle at the ambush and riding from there into the woods. Her account of her struggle with the bear was smooth and full of exciting details. When she finished, she told of raids she had been on with Broken Foot after her mother died. She stopped abruptly. "Moonflower's life has not been exciting like Eagle's." She touched his arm with her hand.

He took both her hands in his. "You are as lovely as the flower of your name. That is enough." They walked quietly back to their horses, feeling glad to be together. Before riding back to the village, they made brief plans to meet secretly during the Hunting Dance.

The village was buzzing with excitement that evening, even though it was still three days before the first summer buffalo hunt, which involved the whole community. Everyone's enthusiasm was building as he or she made various kinds of preparations. For three straight nights there would be the Hunting Dance to celebrate the good times to come. The dances were held in the great circle, usually around a big fire; tonight a fire was not necessary because of the summer weather and a full moon.

When Eagle arrived at the dance, eight singers and eight drummers were beginning the entertainment. Unmarried men of the village who were lined up on one side of the circle were preparing to cross over and select partners from the line of maidens on the other side. Most of the participants were joining in the singing. Eagle enjoyed watching the dance, which would go on for hours. He seldom participated and was not expected to this evening.

After watching a few minutes, he drifted back behind the other spectators and made his way to Standing Buck's tepee, which was just behind Broken Foot's and not easily seen by passersby. Standing Buck had moved there while waiting for his power. He needed to be away from his sister and from the contamination of cooking fat. Because his power had come to him with the rising of the full moon, Moonflower knew he would be at the dance, at least until midnight, so she had suggested his tepee for a tryst.

"Moonflower," he called softly, trying to keep the excitement from his voice. His anticipation was greater than he had felt before claiming the great white horses he won from Coyote Droppings.

She was not there. He controlled his disappointment and slipped inside to wait. Perhaps she had been assigned a difficult chore and had not finished. Surely, she would not forget their meeting. He did not want to think about rejection. Unspoken and unbreakable pledges had passed between them in the afternoon—at least he thought so.

The moon was high when Eagle gave up and returned dejectedly to his tepee. Perhaps he had been right. Perhaps one would do better to spend his time in prayer and meditation than to give his heart to a woman. When he tried to pray, Moonflower was all he could think about. He wanted her. He needed her.

He decided to forgive her, no matter why she missed the meeting. She was young. He would use the patience he had developed as a warrior and wait to see if she made amends. If she did not, he had the spiritual discipline to forget her and lose himself again in hunting and raiding. After the communal hunt, which he always enjoyed enormously, he would lead a raid above the River Colored by Clay. That would be a good summer's project.

Some time after he had finally gone to sleep, he heard her voice and thought he was dreaming. He heard it again whispering urgently, "Eagle!" He stumbled to the door and folded back the flap. The moon, which had descended from its highest point for the night, highlighted her beauty better than did the sun.

"You are truly a moon flower," he said, as she rushed into his arms.

"Broken Foot wanted me to go to the Hunting Dance with Takes a Chance. When I refused, he would not let me leave the tepee. I slipped out after he finally fell asleep. He said he plans to negotiate a marriage with Takes a Chance even if I object." She hugged him tightly. "Save me! Takes a Chance is an old man, and he has a mean wife. Moonflower would be miserable in his tepee."

Eagle, always decisive in battle, was confused. All he could offer was silence.

"Keep me here tonight. I will be your wife."

Eagle thought a moment as she clung to him. The words were hard to say. "Eagle cannot do this. It would not be honorable."

"People often elope. You have many horses. You could give compensation." When she said it, she knew they were the wrong words for this man.

"That is not the way of leaders. Eagle must honor the covenant Broken Foot has made with Takes a Chance."

"Even if Moonflower must suffer for it?" She knew the answer. Honor was more important than anything else.

He held her away. "I will talk to Broken Foot when Father Sun is high in the sky tomorrow. You must go back to Broken Foot's tepee before you are missed."

Tears streamed from her eyes as she turned to leave. Eagle resisted the urge to call her back. He sat and lit a pipe. He would be unable to sleep anymore that night. He would make medicine.

Part 3:
THE MARRIAGE

Broken Foot, though he had seen fewer than fifty winters, looked like an old man, stooped and slow moving. His mind was still young, but he knew he would not fight anymore. For excitement he would have to spend the rest of his days smoking and telling stories in the smoke lodge with the old warriors.

His physical problems had come as the aftermath of a mysterious disease he had contracted while a prisoner of the Tonkawa to the south. It was a disease they had caught from the Spaniard. It had killed many of them and broken the health of others. When Broken Foot survived, the Tonkawa set him free, believing his recovery was a sign from the Great Spirit.

For awhile he continued to ride with the other warriors and was known for his daredevil antics in battle. Sensing his rapid deterioration, he took even greater risks, preferring death in battle to dying in his tepee. His war medicine was too great, however; and over the past year he had found it necessary to remain behind when his friends rode out.

The sun burned down from a clear, blue sky when Eagle made his way to Broken Foot's tepee. The older warrior, wearing only a breech-cloth, was sitting in front of his tepee. His muscles sagged like those of a much older man. Moonflower was nearby working on some handsome buckskin leggings. Eagle guessed they were for Broken Foot to wear in the communal hunt. He admired the workmanship and wished they were his.

"Broken Foot is honored by a visit from a great war chief." He invited Eagle to sit before him and offered him the pipe he had just lit.

Eagle puffed and then returned the pipe. It tasted of oak leaves, not good tobacco. "Eagle would like to make a great gift to Broken Foot."

Broken Foot looked at him intently. "Umm."

"Eagle's successes have made him a wealthy man. He would like to share this wealth with Broken Foot."

Broken Foot's eyes twinkled slightly, "Why would Broken Foot deserve such wealth?"

"Broken Foot has a daughter." He looked at Moonflower, who nodded encouragement.

Broken Foot shook his head sadly, obviously sorry to disappoint Eagle and lose the wealth besides. "After the hunt she will belong to Takes a Chance."

Eagle nodded and rose to leave. Broken Foot held out his hand indicating Eagle should remain awhile longer. "Eagle spoke of a great gift." He handed Eagle the pipe.

Eagle sat again and unrolled a square of buckskin, which he placed on his back to protect it from the sun. "Broken Foot has ridden the warrior's road but seldom since returning from the Tonkawa. His herd is small." He took a puff from the pipe. It was getting strong and bitter. "Broken Foot's young son has not brought home many horses or other prizes." He looked at the pipe and handed it back. He avoided mentioning that Broken Foot was not likely to ride with a war party again. It was understood between them.

Eagle observed, "Takes a Chance does not have a large herd, and he can not fight many more years. His medicine is weak. It would be far better for Broken Foot to have a wealthy young war chief for a son. Such a son could take care of him until he is *ready* to ride to the Great Spirit's hunting grounds." They both knew cripples without influential family were sometimes left behind to die when their band decided to migrate.

Broken Foot shifted his legs. "Eagle has not named the gift."

"Twenty fine horses that have been bred and trained by Talks to Horses."

Broken Foot's eyes sparkled. "Broken Foot has made promises to Takes a Chance. Broken Foot would suffer much dishonor."

"Twenty of such horses are more than any father has ever received in Eagle's memory."

"For such a woman as this." Broken Foot pointed dramatically at Moonflower. "A hundred horses would not be too much!"

Eagle kept his eyes on Broken Foot. "What gift has Takes a Chance offered?"

Broken Foot disregarded the question. "There is the problem of dishonor to be considered." Broken Foot laid his pipe aside and spit some of the bitterness onto the ground. "Broken Foot could bear dishonor if he had a fine white horse to ride in the hunt."

Eagle almost laughed. Now he knew that this was all a game. Of course, Broken Foot was not going to give his daughter to Takes a Chance. He, and perhaps Standing

Buck, had devised a scheme to get Whirlwind from Eagle. Broken Foot had never owned such a fine animal and could never hope to catch one. Talks to Horses had bred him from the ponies Eagle had claimed when he killed Coyote Droppings. He was as fast and as smart as any horse Eagle had seen, including Talks to Horses' great mustang, Night Wind. All the other warriors admired Whirlwind, and Eagle loved him.

He knew Broken Foot intended Moonflower for him, and he could call the older warrior's bluff, but there were other factors to consider. Eagle was wealthy and respected. To make a generous gift would increase his prestige. It would show he believed in his medicine. The horses, including his war horse, could be replaced. In fact, he had his eye on a black and white paint sired by Night Wind. He could be the fastest horse ever to come from Talks to Horses' herd.

Eagle looked at Moonflower. She was worth a magnificent gift.

"Ask any other horse," said Eagle adamantly.

"Broken Foot yearns for a fine white one."

"It cannot be!"

"Such a horse would make Broken Foot forget his shame."

"Broken Foot would not be satisfied with him. Talks to Horses has an exceptional black and white one that is much better, much faster."

Broken Foot offered Eagle the pipe. "There can be no marriage without the white horse."

Eagle reluctantly took the pipe. "Then Broken Foot will have Whirlwind and twenty fine horses." Eagle rose majestically, his expression somber, and strode from Broken Foot's tepee. But as he left, his eyes met Moonflower's. The look he gave her made a blush stain her face, and she bent her head to hide her delighted smile.

That evening when Eagle delivered the horses to Broken Foot's herd, he killed a small roan, and cut out the heart. This he took to Moonflower's tepee and hung it beside the flap; then he returned to his tepee.

After she had roasted the heart, she divided it into two portions and took them to his tepee. When he opened the flap, she announced, "Moonflower returns the heart Eagle gave her." Her hair was braided with blue ribbons, and she was wearing a pretty doeskin dress Morning Dove had made and decorated. In her right hand she held an earthen bowl with the roasted heart; in her left were the leggings he had seen her making earlier.

Eagle ate dinner with his wife in their tepee.

THE BIRTH

PART 1:
GETTING READY

Moonflower lay beside Eagle on the buffalo-hide bed, her head nestled in the crook of his arm. He had just returned from an arduous but successful raid on the Pawnee far to the north. The fall evenings were cold on the plains, and the comforts of his own tepee and being with his beautiful wife gave him a feeling of euphoria. Even though they had been married for two winters, the sweetness of being with her had not diminished—it had increased.

After he had recounted the raid on the Pawnee, she was quiet for a few moments and then, "Would it please you if Moonflower gave you a baby?"

He tightened his arm around her shoulder. "Yes! Especially if it were a little warrior."

Excitement rose in her voice. "I have talked with Morning Dove. She thinks the baby will come at the end of spring." Her sister had two sons and had helped with the births of several other children. She would be Moonflower's constant adviser and helper during her pregnancy.

For the next few weeks Eagle was happy with thoughts about the coming child. It would bring even more joy to his life, and when Eagle was dead, he would live on through his son.

Then Moonflower began to have sickness and great pains in her abdomen. He knew of many miscarriages and also deaths among the Comanche mothers, and the anxiety from this knowledge destroyed his joy and took him to Morning Dove's tepee. She was kneeling just inside the flap, sewing on a baby's shirt.

"Will Moonflower give birth to this baby?" He knelt beside her.

Tears flooded Morning Dove's eyes, and she shook her head. "It is bad. Moonflower's body is not built well for bearing children. Her hips are narrow."

"And so this baby may take her life?"

"It was so with Fallen Leaf and others of The People."

For the next few days Eagle's spirit was heavy with sorrow and dread. He asked Morning Dove to stay with Moonflower while he went away to spend two full days in prayer on the Hump of the Buffalo, where he had received his first vision. He asked the Great Spirit to spare Moonflower's life and to send him a boy. He promised to make a great warrior of him to follow in his footsteps and the footsteps of his fathers before him.

The Great Spirit sent no vision to relieve his anxiety. However, he did develop a strong feeling that he should take a chore wife. Even while she was sick, Moonflower worked diligently to make him comfortable and happy. She tanned hides, made handsome clothes and robes, cared for his horses, made delicious meals and looked to his every need and wish. All this was without complaint, though he knew she was often in pain. Added to all that were her preparations for the coming of the baby. And then later, when the baby came—he refused to say *if*—caring for him would take even more time, and there was no mother or mother-in-law to help out.

Willow had died of a lung disease two winters earlier. Morning Dove would help some, but she had responsibilities of her own. No, another wife was needed, he thought. Not only would she be a help to Moonflower, but also she would enhance his status and reflect his wealth. He had over three hundred horses but only one wife.

Since Moonflower had no younger sisters for him to choose from, he kept his eyes open for a suitable prospect within the village. He found none right away and was soon distracted by preparations for the fall communal hunt. When he thought of the idea again, he wondered if it were a good one. Moonflower was the best wife he had ever seen, and he loved her deeply. Another wife in the tepee might change their relationship. What if he selected someone whom Moonflower would dislike or feel threatened by? What might that do to her health? Might it even affect the baby in her womb?

Just before winter, Eagle and some other warriors took a small herd of horses to trade with a band of friendly Wichita just above the Beaver River. They were good farmers and usually had a surplus of corn, tobacco, and other farm products to trade for horses. The Antelope band, on the other hand, had plenty of horses, but raised nothing, depending primarily on their hunting and whatever vegetable products grew wild, such as pecans, wild plums, persimmons, mesquite beans, and prickly pears.

The Wichita farmers were happy to see the Antelope warriors, as they had reaped good harvests and had a large surplus for trade. They wanted to know right away which were Eagle's horses and, of those, which had been bred by Talks to Horses. They knew these would be the best.

Trading in the Wichita village was carried on in a big open space beside their thatched, dome-shaped dwellings. Those of the Wichita who had food products for trade brought them for display. Eagle examined large skin bags full of wheat, smaller bags full of tobacco, and baskets full of corn. As Eagle walked along the row of products, the growers examined his horses. When Eagle saw something he wanted, he stood before it waiting for the owner to return from looking at the horses and propose a barter.

While Eagle was examining bags of tobacco, he was approached by an older Wichita grower, who had been eyeing a handsome pair of brown and white mustangs. The Wichita was almost as tall as Eagle and had long unbraided black hair streaked with gray. He wore a buckskin shirt, a loin cloth of bear skin, and moccasins with leggings. His mouth turned up in a slight smile when he talked. "Black Leg will trade some of the finest corn ever grown for the pair of brown and white mustangs." In a big calloused hand he held an ear of yellow corn with the shucks pulled back.

Eagle shook his head. "Eagle has already traded for corn. He needs tobacco."

"Black Leg has no tobacco this year." He looked hungrily at the mustangs. A half dozen other growers were stroking the horses and examining their mouths. "Black Leg has traded with Eagle and the Antelope for many winters. He knows Eagle to be a worthy war chief. For this reason, he will offer him one of his beautiful daughters for the mustangs and that big grey next to them."

104

Eagle looked over at the horses indifferently. "Eagle is a great warrior. He can find many willing wives among the beautiful Antelope maidens."

The old warrior countered. "Wichita women are hard workers, and they are passionate." He gave Eagle a knowing look.

Eagle smiled faintly and said as though to humor Black Leg, "Where are these passionate women?"

Black Leg led him across the market area to a lean-to full of corn. Sitting beside it gnawing meat from buffalo ribs were three fat, sullen women, wearing straight buckskin dresses that went from their necks to below their knees. Black Leg made them stand for Eagle to inspect. He examined them carefully as he would examine horses, even looking at their teeth. They were dirty and smelled bad.

Eagle stood back, shaking his head. "Are there others?"

Black Leg started to negotiate, but Eagle held up his hand to indicate he had no interest in a trade. Black Leg looked longingly at the brown and white mustangs and whispered something in the biggest daughter's ear. She wiped her mouth on her sleeve and trudged off. In a few minutes she returned with another Wichita maiden.

As Eagle had suspected, she was to them as the blue bird is to the buzzard. She was a small, pretty girl of about seventeen winters. She wore a shorter dress than her sisters. When he looked into her eyes, she smiled shyly. He thought he understood her plight when he took one of her rough calloused hands. It was much rougher than those of her sisters. As the youngest and the smallest, she had to do most of the work for her sisters and their mothers. That would also explain their obesity.

Though she was shy, she met and held Eagle's gaze. Seeing courage and determination in her eyes, his heart went out to her. If she were a man, he believed she would be a fine warrior. "This one," he said to Black Leg, taking her small arm.

"For Little Robin, Black Leg would have to receive much more than the three mustangs." His eyes sparkled with expectation.

"She is small," Eagle observed.

Black Leg shook his head. "Her body is small, but she is pretty and can outwork two women." He glanced at the other daughters, who had sat back down to gnaw the ribs. "Three."

Eagle guessed he might use the extra horses as a dowry to entice suitors for one or two of his remaining daughters. He gave Black Leg the brown and white Mustangs plus three other of his best horses for Little Robin.

Little Robin quickly gathered up her few possessions when it was time to leave; and she shed no tears of farewell, though she hugged Black Leg lovingly. On the trip to her new home, she used sign language and what Antelope words she knew to tell Eagle her mother had died in childbirth, and there was no one to protect her as she grew up. Consequently, she not only had to do most of the undesirable chores but also took considerable abuse from her sisters and her two stepmothers. She indicated that Eagle's fame as a warrior had spread among the Wichita; and she was honored to be his wife, even if she was not to be the main wife. She promised to work hard and be a credit to his name.

Eagle was pleased with Little Robin, even though he had not planned to take a wife from the Wichita. The marriage would not be popular with his people; however, they would accept it because she was merely a chore wife, and because Eagle wanted to do it. No one would dare challenge his actions. An especial benefit of the marriage was that he avoided the family commitments a warrior took on when he married within the Antelope band.

Moonflower was less than happy to see Eagle return with another wife. For two years she had been the sole recipient of his attentions, and she alone had shared the glory of his successful exploits and growing reputation. While she did not abuse Little Robin, she was cool toward her.

Eagle was not surprised to see that Little Robin accepted Moonflower's coolness. She was used to coping with the disapproval of other women. In fact, she was always cheerful and jumped at every opportunity to be helpful to Moonflower, who found her to be as capable as she was willing. While she lacked Moonflower's artistic talent, she never lacked energy and enthusiasm; and she openly admired Moonflower, almost as much as she did Eagle.

The affability of Little Robin combined with her constant concern for Moonflower, who suffered constant pain, finally influenced her to accept Little Robin into her heart. She taught Little Robin the Antelope language and gave her the love and friendship she had not received from her own family.

For awhile, the three of them lived in Eagle's tepee. A buffalo robe formed a partition between Little Robin's bed and the one Eagle shared with Moonflower. Then, Eagle decided it was time to build a separate tepee for the women. They needed the privacy and extra space to prepare for the baby's coming, and he would gain added prestige with this symbol of his increasing wealth. Besides, he was finding it necessary to spend more time alone making medicine nowadays, because he was gradually accepting greater responsibilities in the protecting and governing of the Antelope band.

Just as Moonflower and Robin would have to take care of the tepee and move it when the Antelope moved to new hunting grounds, they would also have to see to its building. They were excited about their new home and discussed it for a long time before finally consulting with Greyfoot, who was the best tepee-maker in the band. In exchange for a suitable gift, a brown mustang with white stockings, she would direct the whole project. Moonflower had helped build several tepees, so she was able to describe in detail what was wanted. With all three women working together, they finished it by the time the coldest weather set in. They made the tepee of twelve tanned buffalo hides and sixteen twelve-foot cedar poles, six fewer than Eagle's had.

The only furniture for the tepee was two beds made from buffalo robes. These were stretched across a frame of cedar poles and rawhide slats. They were elevated about a hand's width above the ground and were comfortable for couches as well as beds. As time drew near for the birth, Little Robin dug two shallow pits in the center of the tepee. The larger one would be filled with hot coals for steaming, and the other would be a receptacle for the after-birth. Little Robin drove two stakes about four feet long into the ground near the pit for coals.

Moonflower grew so large Eagle was afraid she would burst. She rubbed bear grease on her swollen abdomen and stomach to make her stretched skin more elastic, and she drank a dark-colored liquid for her badly swollen feet. Toward the end of spring the baby became extremely active and kept her awake most of the night with its painful kicking and moving around in her womb. Fearing the worst, Eagle called off a spring raid he was planning below the Stinking Buffalo River.

Part 2:
GIVING BIRTH

It was a cool morning after a storm when Moonflower's labor pains began. She instructed Little Robin to prepare the coal pit and then go for Morning Dove and the midwife, Swam the River. Little Robin also alerted Eagle, Long Lance, and Broken Foot, though men would not be permitted in the tepee, unless a medicine man was required.

By midafternoon the labor pains were at short intervals and intense. Moonflower lay on a bed in the humid tepee and quietly endured the pain. Her three women attendants, who kept the coals steaming and occasionally gave her warm soup or water, sat near her and sang doleful songs.

When the pain became almost unbearable, Swam the River required her to get up and squat over the steaming pit, grasping the cedar stakes. "Push." she ordered. While Moonflower forced herself not to cry with the pain and pushed as hard as she could bear to, Swam the River pressed hot rocks to her back.

The baby refused to be born.

Little Robin helped poor Moonflower back to bed, and Morning Dove served her hot soup made from buffalo broth. The pains subsided for awhile and then came back stronger. Moonflower could not help crying out with the pain. Swam the River ordered her to squat over the pit again. This time she chanted a song and then grasped Moonflower's abdomen and squeezed downward. "Push!" she cried. "Push!"

Moonflower fainted this time. When she awakened Morning Dove and Little Robin had laid her on the bed, where she lay pale and drenched with perspiration. At frequent intervals she would writhe with pain. Swam the River shook her head.

Morning Dove tenderly wiped perspiration from her sister's brow and looked questioningly at Swam the River.

"My medicine is not strong enough," she said.

Morning Dove turned to Little Robin, who was holding Moonflower's hand, "Get Whitewater!"

Whitewater was the most effective and most respected medicine man in the Antelope band. Though the Great Spirit had given him big buffalo medicine, he rarely depended on it when a mundane remedy was available. He said Mother Earth had provided things to heal ordinary illnesses and wounds. His buffalo power was for the extraordinary.

Most of the time he used herbs and plants that grew nearby. Sometimes he asked Talks to Horses to find needed substances during his explorations. He made an effective laxative from the cambium layer of the willow tree; he treated toothaches with a mushroom poultice; he made soothing ointments for burns and certain kinds of sores from petroleum he had discovered in a puddle near the river; he treated diarrhea with a scorched wheat-flour paste; he provided an effective cure for stomach ache with a white chalky substance, which he had discovered at Rainfall Mountain and mixed with powdered buffalo stomachs; and he had numerous other remedies.

Some of his treatments required surgery or physical manipulation. He maintained headaches were caused by an evil spirit. He cured them by covering the patient with a buffalo robe, chanting a song, blowing into the patient's mouth and then wrapping his arms around the patient's head and body and popping his or her neck. He had saved the life of his own brother, who had been disemboweled by a Ute knife. Whitewater reinserted the bowel and sewed up the wound with an awl and buffalo sinew.

He also operated on animals. When Long Lance's horse was seriously injured by an enemy spear, Whitewater packed the bleeding wound with grass and wrapped it tightly with white cloth stolen from the Spaniards. The treatment was successful, as were most of his operations. All were preceded by the appropriate buffalo medicine ceremony.

Whitewater was a giant of a man with long, stringy white hair. His wrinkled face was filled with confidence. When he stepped into Moonflower's tepee, she breathed a great sigh of relief. She believed in his medicine and knew her ordeal would soon be over.

He brought three buffalo skins with the tails still attached. He hung one over the door of the tepee and sent another with Little Robin for Eagle to wear. He placed the third over Moonflower, who was thoroughly exhausted but still crying with the excruciating pains.

Whitewater announced, "All will soon be well, little mother." His voice was deep and reassuring. He danced around the two pits four times singing a buffalo song. After this he approached Moonflower, whose color was returning.

"Stand, little mother." He stretched out his hand. Rising with effort, she took it and looked into his eyes. They were dilated. "The power is coming," he assured her. Then he heaved as though to vomit and breathed into her mouth. Moonflower felt the power and stood straight and strong.

"Now squat over the pit, little mother, and take the stakes." He helped her lean over and then turned to Swam the River, took her hand, and spat a mouthful of brownish saliva into it. "Rub that into Moonflower's abdomen. When Whitewater leaves, the baby will drop." He danced around Moonflower four times while Swam the River rubbed in the saliva. Then he abruptly turned to the entrance and jumped through.

The tepee was filled with the cries of a baby. Little Robin helped Moonflower back to her bed. She was trembling with exhaustion, and yet she was excited and renewed. She had borne Eagle a son! She was still alive! Quickly, Morning Dove bathed the baby in warm water, wrapped him in soft rabbit furs, and handed him to Moonflower to hold to her breast for a few moments. She was ecstatic, even the pain from the baby's sucking at her breast excited her. She was giving of herself physically and spiritually. What a fine son he was! She was sure one day he would be a great chief like his father, and she would be part of him.

After Moonflower tired, Morning Dove placed the baby in a cradle she had brought for the occasion. Swam the River took the umbilical cord from the small pit, wrapped it in buckskin, and put it in a hackberry tree just outside the village. It would stay there until it disintegrated, a sign the baby would live a long life. Meanwhile, Morning Dove and Little Robin purified the tepee by burning sage. When Swam the River returned, they all sang happy songs of life and birth.

Part 3:
NAMING THE BABY

Long Lance was the first man to see the baby and ascertain that he was a boy in good health. Eagle was permitted to see his wife and baby a week later. The name he brought was provided by Long Lance, who had received a vision in which Eagle and then his son after him rose to greatness. After the vision he walked out into the warm night air and saw a shooting star.

"Is he not big and handsome?" Moonflower pointed proudly to the baby when Eagle stepped into her tepee. He was lying naked on a buffalo robe, and Little Robin was gently sponging him off with the same cotton cloth Morning Dove had used to mop Moonflower's brow. Moonflower held him up for Eagle's inspection.

"He is big and handsome!" Eagle put a loving arm around her and the baby. "His name is Shooting Star. He will be a great warrior."

THE VENGEANCE RAID

PART 1: GETTING READY

Eagle watched the hunting party ride quietly into the village, their faces painted black. Eight hunters had ridden out; seven were returning. The first rider was Runs Slow, not Standing Buck. Now Broken Foot had lost all three sons.

During the third consecutive week of cold, icy weather, the hunters had ridden out wrapped in buffalo robes, with Standing Buck the leader. Now, a week later, the weather was as warm as late spring. The hunters wore only breechcloths, enjoying the warmth of the southern sun. It was extremely rare in late winter to have the kind of weather the Comanche had suffered, and he was caught unprepared. He had run out of food and was having to kill horses for food when the hunting parties were finally sent out. Eagle's party had returned seven days ago. The party led by Runs Slow was the last to return.

115

The older people looking on were especially sad and repeated the Comanche proverb, "The brave die young." It would be the blackest day of Broken Foot's life—worse than when he lost his first son in the war with the Tonkawa. Standing Buck had seen only twenty-two winters and was a brave warrior. He was a great source of pride, as well as security, to his father; and now that Broken Foot was too old and crippled to raise more warriors, the tragedy was magnified.

Eagle went with Runs Slow to Broken Foot's tepee. The old warrior had already heard the news and was sitting solemnly beside the entrance with an unlit pipe in his hand. He nodded to the two warriors to sit. "Tell Broken Foot how his son died."

Eagle sat beside Broken Foot, and Runs Slow sat before him. "Standing Buck was killed yesterday," said Runs Slow. "The hunting party found a deer herd after a week of nothing. We killed ten of them. After we had loaded them onto the extra horses, we rode right into a Ute ambush.

"If one of the Ute warriors had not shot early and ruined their ambush, we might all have been killed. Instead all but Standing Buck escaped. He stayed to help Hawk's Nose, whose horse was killed. If he had not done this, the Ute would have the scalp of Hawk's Nose now. Ten Ute warriors came from the trees to kill Hawk's Nose. With his lance Standing Buck killed three of them and fought fiercely with seven more while Hawk's Nose caught one of the Ute horses.

"When they were ready to ride away, three Ute bowmen joined the fight, and one put an arrow in the chest of Standing Buck. Even with the arrow in his chest, Standing Buck outrode the Ute. We buried him on the side of a hill facing the morning sun, and we stacked rocks high on his grave. We killed his favorite white horse for him to ride to the Great Spirit's hunting grounds." Runs Slow rose to his feet. "The Ute took the extra horses and all but two deer."

Broken Foot nodded his thanks and got up slowly, looking to the east. He went into his tepee and sat quietly alone until Eagle brought his weeping daughters, Morning Dove and Moonflower. Then Eagle went to his own tepee to endure his sorrow for this lost friend who was like a brother to him. Standing Buck had hunted with him and fought at his side in numerous raids. The winter before, he had saved Eagle's life when they were ambushed by the Apache.

In late afternoon Broken Foot went to the tepee of Eagle, who was expecting him. The old warrior sat down slowly and filled his pipe. No words were spoken. He lit the pipe carefully and took a long deep pull on it. As the smoke rose to the opening in the top of the tepee, he offered the pipe to Eagle. Acceptance of the pipe would mean Eagle agreed to lead a vengeance raid.

Eagle accepted the pipe and puffed.

"Why would the Ute go so far into the Antelope hunting ground?" asked Broken Foot.

"Horses and food. With bad weather the game has moved this way." Eagle handed the pipe back after his fourth puff. "He will not stay long after this ambush, though." He went to the entrance of his tepee and gave instructions to his nephew, Wild Horse, to find volunteers who could leave at once.

"Broken Foot's heart longs to go," said the old warrior when Eagle sat back down. "The hurt is deep."

Eagle nodded. "It is right that Broken Foot should go, but it cannot be. The vengeance party will have to ride hard all night to catch the Ute."

"Broken Foot understands. That is why he asks Eagle to go for him. Do not fail." He looked hard into Eagle's eyes.

"Eagle will return with a Ute scalp, or he will not return at all."

When Broken Foot left, Eagle sat with legs crossed in the middle of his tepee to make medicine. He unfolded a hide taken from a big buck. His antlers had sixteen points. With these antlers in front of him he wrapped himself in the hide and smoked his sacred pipe. After that he sang prayer songs while he beat softly on a drum made of buckskin; next he prayed to the Great Spirit for power; finally, when he felt the power, he sat meditatively. It was during this time he experienced the Great Spirit's presence and had a strong feeling that the Spirit would ride with him to destroy the Ute.

After he had spent two hours making medicine, he went to Moonflower's tepee. She had roasted a side of one of the deer brought in by Runs Slow. Since meat from a buck was a taboo for Eagle, she had examined the carcass carefully to make sure it was a doe. When he had eaten his fill, the remainder would go to Broken Foot.

She sat quietly beside him while he ate hungrily. He had received strong medicine, and his enthusiasm was high. Though he said almost nothing before a raid, he always insisted Moonflower be at his side. His soul fed on her beauty and sweet companionship. This time, however, he felt her pain because of her brother. After the meal he held her tightly in his arms for a long time, knowing he had no words to comfort her. After he was gone, she would cry loudly and bitterly.

When it was almost time to go, he asked, "Where is Shooting Star?"

"Little Robin has taken him to Talks to Horses. He is teaching our son about horses. He will return before long." As soon as she said it, the child burst through the door with a tearful Little Robin right behind. She ran to Moonflower, and they embraced.

Shooting Star announced, "Today I rode one of the big horses alone! For a long time!" He turned to Little Robin. "Is it not so?"

Little Robin wiped at her eyes and smiled. "It is so. He is a great rider."

Eagle looked proudly at his son. "Could it be that Shooting Star after only four winters can ride like a man?"

"Yes!" He puffed out his chest.

Eagle picked up his son. "Shooting Star will be a great warrior."

"When?"

Eagle said with mock seriousness, "Before many more winters have passed." He set the boy down and said, placing his hands on Shooting Star's shoulders. "Eagle is going on a raid. He will be gone awhile and leaves Shooting Star to take care of his mother and Little Robin." Eagle bent to receive his son's embrace.

Shooting Star was a handsome boy, unusually tall and muscular for his age. "Be sure to come back. Red Wing's father did not come back today." He looked anxiously at Eagle.

"Eagle always comes back. Now go with Little Robin and tell Broken Foot how you rode the horse. We have work to do here." He patted his son on the head and turned to his chore wife.

Little Robin also embraced Eagle. Though still a small woman, she had filled out and was even prettier than when Eagle brought her home from the Wichita village four years ago. "May the Great Spirit protect you." She took the basket of food Moonflower handed her and followed Shooting Star. She looked back to see Eagle one more time before slipping through the door.

Earlier, Moonflower had prepared everything Eagle would need for the raid. Now she helped him apply war paint. First, she parted his black hair down the middle and plaited two braids that came to his shoulders. She left a scalp lock at the back of his head. Then she painted the part red and tied the ends of the braids with softened buckskin. In the scalp lock she placed a brown and white eagle feather that drooped backward and downward. Looking into a brightly polished silver plate he had bought from the Comancheros, Eagle painted his face with a brilliant vermillion and added slanted stripes of yellow and black to his cheeks.

Part 2: THE RAID

Usually before a vengeance raid the village had a big dance lasting five or six hours to give importance and prestige to the project. Tonight, however, it was essential to leave as soon after sunset as possible. A three quarters moon would give adequate light to travel by.

Eagle was sure this Ute hunting party would be on its way back home, and he planned an intersecting course. If he

missed them, he would have to travel farther north than he cared to at this time of the year with only the twenty warriors he had selected for the raid.

He was confident he could catch the Ute, since he would almost certainly return home along a trail most often used by visitors from the north. The trail was to the east of Comanche country and ran north to the River Colored by Clay and south to the Spanish missions. It was established many winters ago by Spanish traders. The Spaniard had disappeared, but not the trail. Eagle believed the Ute party that attacked Standing Buck was part of a larger group heading north. Probably in their eagerness to find deer, they had wandered farther west than the Ute leaders would have permitted. He believed the attack on The People had not been approved, and now the Ute wanted to get away before he suffered retaliation.

Even before his meeting with Broken Foot about this raid, Eagle had talked with Runs Slow to find out all he could. Then he sent out six scouts in pairs to look for the Ute at different points north of where the attack occurred. He would lead the rest of the raiders to a rendezvous point on the Blue Water River.

They rode hard all night and reached the rendezvous point an hour before dawn. Eagle, wrapped in his buckskin blanket, slept soundly until wakened at dawn by mockingbirds chasing a squirrel. They were in a grove of live oaks at a fork of the river. It was a spot where The People had won a decisive victory over the Ute five winters before. Though the grass was brown, the bright blue of the water, and the warmth of the sun gave a sense of spring. There were fresh deer tracks along the river bank, and the raiders wanted to hunt some for their breakfast. Before organizing the hunt, Eagle sent out six scouts with instructions to ride hard and return by dark. Shortly after they left, a pair of the scouts he had sent out the afternoon before arrived, their horses exhausted.

Three Crows and Bent Shield had experienced very little difficulty in finding the Ute trail half a day's ride to the south. From the top of a hill they had seen fifty warriors driving a herd of at least a hundred horses. Eagle and Talks to Horses looked at each other with mutual excitement when they heard of the horses; taking a scalp suddenly became a little less important. Capturing those horses from fifty warriors would be an exciting challenge for Eagle and his twenty raiders. He would have to plan carefully.

By dark all the scouts had arrived at the rendezvous point. After a dinner of venison, the warriors, wrapped in buffalo robes, sat in a circle in the moonlight and passed the sacred pipe Eagle carried on all raids. As the pipe passed, Eagle listened to the information and advice each warrior offered. Then he added all the information he had and went over his plan of attack carefully and thoroughly. After the warriors knew exactly where to go and what to do, they joined in songs and prayers directed to the Great Spirit, invoking his aid for the next day's attack.

The following afternoon Talks to Horses, riding his favorite war horse, Night Wind, led five other warriors to their positions. The spot Eagle had chosen for the ambush was along Hundred Rock Creek, which the Ute would have to cross if he stayed on the trail. Though the water was shallow, the crossing was a good two hundred feet wide and extremely rocky. It was a difficult place for horses to maneuver easily.

The warriors hid themselves and their horses in the trees and dead brush along the north bank. They were so skilled at hiding and camouflaging that not even the animals that happened along the creek detected them.

Five of Eagle's oldest and most seasoned veterans were with Talks to Horses, because surprise was absolutely essential to the day's success. Eagle did not want a perfect ambush spoiled by an overly eager warrior, as had happened with the Ute attack on Standing Buck.

The veterans waited patiently as the Ute warriors drove the horses ahead of them into the water. They were relaxed and unconcerned about attack. Some were taking off their buckskin shirts to better enjoy the warm sun on their backs. They shouted jokes at one another while the horses bent their heads and drank thirstily. It had been a successful trip, and they were already anticipating a triumphant return to their village.

Most of the Ute warriors were in the water when Talks to Horses and his ambushers shot their first volley of arrows. The farthest Ute was less than a hundred feet away, too close for a veteran warrior to miss his target. Instantly, six Ute warriors fell screaming from their horses. Before the others could take effective evasive measures, six more died.

Finally realizing what was happening, most of the remaining enemy made for the trees east and west of the Antelope's position. They would try to surround the attackers. Seeing what the Ute planned, Talks to Horses and his warriors jumped on their horses, and with loud war cries to signal the others, they raced northward. As Eagle had hoped, about half the Ute force joined in the chase, leaving the rest to keep the herd together.

With the Ute's attention focused on the north bank and on keeping the horses from running off, Eagle and his warriors moved into position on the south side. The Ute's herd, which Eagle saw was mostly the kind the Spanish had sold or traded to bands in the south, were frightened by the screaming and were trying to break away. Before the Ute could regain control, Eagle implemented the next stage of his ambush. He knew the group chasing Talks to Horses would be out of earshot now; he also figured his brother and the other Antelope warriors would need no help. A Ute could not hope to match a Comanche horseman, especially when his horse was fresh.

When Eagle gave the signal, fourteen bows twanged, and twelve Utes pitched from their horses; two had more than one arrow in their bodies. The other Ute riders, already nervous from the first attack, sprang for the north shore. Six more screamed and fell before they could reach safety. Eagle let the other three or four go. His main interest was capturing the horses, and they were beginning to gallop off in all directions.

"Get the horses back to the other side!" he shouted. "As many as you can!" He knew most of these horses would be fast and well trained. As he moved in among them, he recognized those taken from Standing Buck, but he let them go and chased an exceptional roan horse. Its rider had an arrow between his shoulder blades and was barely hanging on. Eagle quickly overtook the horse as the Ute fell lifeless to the ground. Eagle dismounted and as he took the scalp yelled, "Aiee!" This one would be enough to satisfy Broken Foot, and it could be used for the Scalp Dance.

Eagle guessed the other Ute warriors would soon give up the chase and return for the horses; and though the numbers were about even, he did not want a head-to-head battle that would cost the lives of some of his warriors. With a scalp and almost fifty horses, he was content to go home. He yelled, "Go to Bear Rock!" It was the previously agreed on rendezvous point, where they would meet Talks to Horses and his party.

When the Ute warriors reassembled at the creek, they could choose between counterattacking or gathering up the rest of the horses and going home. Being still far from home and not having significantly superior numbers, they would, Eagle felt sure, choose to gather up and go home. To be safe, however, he left two scouts behind to bring word if there was a counterattack.

All the scouts arrived at Bear Rock by dark with word there was no pursuit. Talks to Horses brought a prisoner. Clad in a breech-cloth, leggings, and moccasins, his body showed no signs he had been in a fight. During the evening meeting around the fire while the warriors counted coup, Talks to Horses counted his coup.

"Twelve of the Ute chased six Antelope warriors. The older ones knew they could not catch us and turned back. The young foolish ones kept after us. That is when the Antelope turned to face the Ute warriors. They were like small dogs fighting a mountain lion. Talks to Horses lanced the leader. Never Stops lanced two more, and Angry Cub shot another from his pony. Two cowards turned and ran while this Ute stayed to fight." The warriors cheered loudly. They knew Talks to Horses had not been on a raid in many winters. He had gone on this one because the Ute had killed Morning Dove's brother. He would return home a hero.

The captive was a tall, slightly fat youth, and he had struggled awkwardly against his captors, unable to make them pay a price in pain for his capture. Even so, he had saved his friends, and the Antelope raiders felt he was a worthy captive. They had him and scalps, too.

Part 3:
THE SCALP DANCE

Eagle timed their return so they arrived near the village two mornings later. He sent in his youngest warrior, Black Feather, with the news that the raid was a success. Meanwhile the warriors reapplied their war paint, put on their war dress, and cleaned the horses, rubbing them with grass.

Eagle led the victory parade into the village with the Ute scalp tied to the end of his lance, which he held high. He was followed by Talks to Horses and his band of five veterans, who proudly guarded the Ute captive. Then came the rest of the warriors and the captured horses.

They were met by another parade marching out from the village. It was led by Standing Buck's widow, Sparrow's Flight, who held a lance high. They were followed by other villagers, mostly women, who sang songs of victory. When the two groups met, Eagle tied the scalp to the widow's lance.

The two groups proceeded together to a scalp pole which had been erected in the center of the village circle. Never Stops and Angry Cub tied the captive to the pole and transferred the scalp from the lance of Sparrow's Flight to the top of the pole. All the victorious warriors then turned their equipment and horses over to their wives or other relatives and went to their tepees to eat and rest for the evening's Scalp Dance and Eagle's dividing the spoils of victory.

During the day the village was filled with yelling and singing. Some of the women assembled a large stack of wood near the scalp pole for the Scalp Dance. Others enjoyed taunting the captive, though Eagle had forbidden them to injure him. He remained silent as the women insulted him, spit in his face, and threw dirt on him. The Ute would have shown no compassion if he had captured an Antelope, and he neither hoped for nor expected any for himself.

The Scalp Dance began at dark. Eagle and the other warriors, wearing only breech-cloths, leggings, and moccasins, appeared in red paint. The women, wearing dresses with brightly colored decorations, were painted with black. Eagle and Talks to Horses wore buffalo headpieces.

When everything was ready, Eagle signaled the singers and drummers to begin. They started the dance with soft music. The dancers, comprised of both men and women, began in a wide circle and danced toward the scalp pole and the captive, tightening the circle as they moved forward. The warriors who had participated in the raid wounded the Ute slightly with their knives when the circle tightened. Variations of this dance continued till nearly midnight, with the music and other noises increasing in tempo and loudness.

At this dance, as at most others, there was a whip holder, who served as leader of the dance. He could point his whip at any spectator and require him to dance; if the person refused, he could be whipped. Toward the end of the dance, he danced over to Broken Foot, who was seated in a position of honor next to Eagle and Talks to Horses.

When he pointed his whip at Broken Foot, the old warrior proudly took a deep breath and forced his debilitated body to walk with poise. The music gave him strength. With his long-bladed knife, he shuffled slowly and menacingly around the Ute, who still had not changed his expression, though his body was bloody. While Broken Foot danced, the singing rose to a deafening pitch.

After he had circled the warrior four times, Broken Foot screamed, "Aiee!" and plunged his knife into the Ute's chest. Standing Buck was avenged.

THE CAPTIVE: JUAN

Juan Horse pulled the entrails from the cow's carcass. Steam rose from them in the early spring morning air. He made a deft cut with his knife and measured off about a foot of bright, white intestines. When he severed it, green oozed from the cut ends. He pinched the top with his thumb and forefinger and pulled downward, forcing the aromatic green mixture out onto the ground. Then he chewed the flattened rope hungrily. This was when it tasted best, still warm and pungent. After chewing most of it, he bent over and cut into the cow's udder. A smoky mixture of milk and blood streamed out. He bent down and drank thirstily.

Eagle, now called Fighting Eagle by The People, was the leader of this raiding party. He approached Juan and said approvingly, "That will make you strong." Juan moved aside to offer Eagle a drink. It was pure white now. He cupped his hand, filled it with milk, and took a long swallow. "Good." He wiped his hand on the long green grass and stood beside Juan, who was looking out across the Mexican ranch land.

Over a hundred warriors dressed in buckskins were divided into smaller groups feasting on twenty-five or thirty freshly killed cattle. A few other carcasses lay untouched, and the rest of the herd was stampeding north, away from Don Mendoza's hacienda. With the back of his hand Juan wiped milk that had dribbled from the right side of his mouth. "When will we attack the casa grande?"

Eagle glanced at the sun. "The afternoon is best. Most of the workers will be away in the fields or chasing after the cows. The ones who stay behind will be sleeping. It is always this way."

This was a day Juan had looked forward to for six years, a day to get revenge on Don Mendoza. He was the biggest rancher-farmer in Chihuahua. Burned into Juan's memory was a day when he was less than ten years old. His father and a group of Don Sanchez's other workers had been contracted to help harvest Don Mendoza's wheat. It was a bright autumn day that began with a family breakfast on a white stone table behind their small adobe home. Juan's mouth watered thinking of his mother's delicious corn tortillas stuffed with mashed beans and green peppers. He and his sister Teresa finished breakfast early and played with a white kitten his father had brought home the night before. It was long-haired and looked like a big ball of cotton. His mother and father drank coffee and laughed at their play. They were a happy family, full of love.

Because Juan was big and strong for his age and every hand was needed to get in the wheat quickly, Don Sanchez sent Juan and several other of the older children along to help. Juan did not yet have the endurance to do a full day's work, and he got fatigued in the warm afternoon sun. He received no pity from Don Mendoza's foreman, Pedro, a short man built like a bull and as mean as the man he worked for. Pedro accused Juan of being lazy and began to lash him with a short whip he carried.

Tears started in Juan's eyes as he thought about his handsome father jumping angrily on the little bull and knocking him to the ground. Pedro's nose was crooked, and blood flowed from it onto his white shirt. His eyes were wide with fear as he yelled for help. Don Mendoza, who was nearby, came to his aid. He hit Juan's father in the back with the butt of a rifle. The blow damaged a kidney that would not heal. He died the next year. Juan's heartbroken mother could not face life without her husband. He was everything to her. She declined into bad health and died a year later. Juan swore the day she died he would kill Don Mendoza.

When Eagle announced his intention to lead a raid into Mexico, Juan readily volunteered. He had forced most of his childhood out of his memory but not Don Mendoza. He remembered everything about the man's fat face and repulsive personality; and he knew about the casa grande and how much wealth it contained. He told Eagle about Don Mendoza, and Eagle was immediately interested—interested in the riches and interested in helping his blood brother get revenge.

Juan stripped back the cowhide and cut off a big flank steak for Eagle and one for himself. They stuck their lances into the steaks and walked to a nearby fire where half a dozen warriors were eating. They quickly made way for Eagle and his brother. The two warriors broiled the meat and then found a clump of soft, green grass to sit on.

"This meat is good," Juan observed. "It is more tender than buffalo, but the flavor is not so good."

Eagle laughed. "Six years ago when Eagle found Juan Horse, he had never eaten fresh meat. Now he is an authority on it."

"We got beef once a year. It was not this color, though." He chewed off a big bite of his steak. "It was green." Juan enjoyed seeing Eagle laugh.

When he started to tell Eagle more about his old diet, he saw that the Antelope war chief was oblivious to the outside world. He was planning the afternoon raid. Juan believed he was a man of true greatness: he had powerful medicine, he loved his people, he was strong and courageous, and he was full of wisdom. Moreover, he had the striking facial features Juan felt hero-leaders should have. He thought Eagle could have been the handsome prince in one of the fairy tales his mother told him long ago.

Juan, who, some said, resembled his great brother, always paid close attention to everything Eagle said and did, hoping to emulate his life. Already, though he was a Mexican and only eighteen, he was highly respected by Eagle and the other Antelope warriors for his skill and courage in battle. Eagle had told him that before many more winters passed, he would be a war chief. Juan would be forever grateful to this man who had saved his life and given him the opportunity to be a great warrior instead of an impoverished worker all his life.

He remembered the day of his capture, which he now thought of as his day of liberation. When he and his sister, Teresa, heard the Comanche coming, they were terrified. They had heard stories of torture and death. It was a winter afternoon, with most of Don Sanchez's men away from the hacienda or asleep. His Grandmother, who was a kitchen maid, was working inside the casa grande. When they heard the war whoops, he ran toward the casa grande with Teresa and her baby, Ana, close behind. They never made it. The raiders swooped down on them and snatched them onto their horses without breaking stride. When he tried to fight, a warrior knocked him unconscious with a club.

Their captors took them, the stolen horses, and other spoils back to their camp and divided everything among themselves. The chiefs got first choice. Eagle chose Juan, and a chief named Kicking Bird claimed Teresa and her baby. Eagle told Juan later he had tried to trade his share of the horses for Teresa, but Kicking Bird was not interested. He was from a neighboring Comanche band, called the Penateka.

The two bands had joined in a war against the Apache and afterwards maintained friendly relations. In the winter the Penateka was running low on horses and traded some white prisoners to the Antelope for horses. At that time Eagle invited their chief, Lone Wolf, to send some warriors along on the raid into Mexico.

The night Kicking Bird claimed Teresa, Eagle heatedly pointed out to him that Lone Wolf had agreed the Antelope could have all prisoners. Since they had a wealth of horses, prisoners were of far more value. Some could be returned for ransom, some could be sold or traded, and others, like Juan, could be taken into the tribe to increase its strength.

Kicking Bird would not cooperate. He wanted the pretty Mexican girl for a wife, and he was willing to fight to keep her. Since the other Antelope leaders had advised Eagle not to squabble with the Penateka chief, he gave in and took Juan, his horses, and the other plunder back across the Stinking Buffalo River. Kicking Bird stayed for more raiding. He later told Eagle the Mexican girl got lost in the desert and died. Eagle believed he killed her.

After his capture Juan decided the raiders were going to kill him no matter what he did; therefore, he never showed any emotion but defiance. Finally, Eagle tied him to a tree, and three warriors prepared as though to shoot him. He spat at them and called them heathen savages. Even when they fired the arrows, which went just over his head, he did not flinch. Impressed by his behavior, Eagle cut him loose. Through an interpreter he told Juan he was a brave young man and could ride the warrior's road one day if he was willing to learn the ways of the Antelope.

Juan was awed by Eagle and flattered by Eagle's faith in him. Besides, he had often admired the freedom of these raiders from the north. He and the other boys had romantic ideas about the Comanche lifestyle and pretended to be raiders themselves sometimes when they played in the evenings. His life on the hacienda was drudgery from morning till evening, just as his father's life had been. If he escaped from the Antelope and returned to his home, Juan would never be anything but a poor worker. So he was happy to become one of The People and never regretted it.

He was fascinated with everything about the life of a warrior and learned to be a skilled hunter and a brave warrior. He loved these activities, but most of all he loved the horses, and he became a friend and admirer of Eagle's brother, Talks to Horses. From him Juan learned everything he could about the animals from breeding them to healing them. Juan knew no one could ride better than The People, and he was determined to surpass all of them.

Eagle kept a close eye on Juan for about a year to be sure he was serious about riding the warrior's road. Then he called a council meeting and conducted a ceremony in which Juan became a Comanche.

The leading chiefs in the Antelope village sat in a circle and passed a pipe. After smoking, they stood up facing the sun. They placed their hands over their hearts and then raised them to the sun. They did this again as they marched around in a circle. Afterward, Eagle sent two young warriors to bring Juan into the circle. There he took an oath of allegiance to Eagle and to the band. Then, they gave him his new name, Juan Horse, and Eagle adopted him as his blood brother. On that day Talks to Horses gave him Night Runner, a pony sired by his own favorite horse, Night Wind.

Juan was lying in the soft grass dreaming about his childhood when Eagle shook his shoulder. "We must go, my brother." As it was a warm afternoon, the warriors would wear only breech-cloths and leggings. They painted their faces, mostly with vermillion, and hung feathers from their scalplocks. Then they mounted their sleek horses and followed Eagle at a gallop toward the casa grande of Don Mendoza.

They approached the casa grande from the rolling hills to the north. Juan was impressed anew with its grandeur. It was comprised of a large adobe building surrounded by smaller ones connected with courtyards and covered patios. It was landscaped with green lawns, flower gardens and giant oak trees. Juan was angered by the thought that these things were built, planted, and tended by poor laborers, all working for the pleasure and comfort of one giant pig of a man, Don Mendoza. Juan's father had said that since Mendoza's wife died years ago, the only women to enjoy the inside of the casa grande were his whores.

Of most interest to the raiders were the stables and corrals south of the casa grande. They held Mendoza's breeding stock, twenty of the finest horses in Mexico. At least forty more fine horses were in the pasture below the corral. Eagle took six warriors with him to the stable, and the rest of his group went into the pasture to collect the herd. If any workers were in the stables, they hid in the loft or in the out-buildings when they heard the raiders' first war whoops, and the cowherds in the pasture ran for the hills.

As he had arranged earlier with Eagle, Juan took three warriors to the main house, where two black horses were tied to a post outside. The saddles were also black and were profusely decorated with silver. Two well-dressed Mexicans ran from the house toward the horses. Then they saw the raiders and fell over themselves getting back inside. A cold rage filled Juan's heart when he recognized Don Mendoza. Juan signaled the other warriors to go around and enter by the other doors. He dismounted and went in the door used by Mendoza and his guest.

Knowing Mendoza would have guns, Juan entered the casa grande cautiously. In his left hand he carried a shield made of dried buffalo hides; it would deflect pistol bullets. In his right hand he gripped a knife with a blade almost a foot long. He pushed a door open into a long, shadowy hallway of Mexican tapestries and varnished walnut doors and woodwork. For Juan it was like entering a doorway into the past. It was similar to Don Sanchez's casa grande, where he had helped his grandmother clean the floors. It evoked feelings and memories he preferred to leave unremembered.

Someone fired shots in the back of the casa grande, and women screamed. Then Juan heard running footsteps. He tried the door to his right. It was a closet. He slipped inside, leaving the door ajar. At the other end of the hall a door opened, and the footsteps ran down the hall toward him. Juan waited until the man had passed his door, and then burst out. It was the man Juan had seen with Mendoza. He was about Juan's size and wore a black and silver suit with a matching wide-brimmed hat.

The man started to spin around, raising the gun in his right hand. He never completed the turn. Juan plunged his knife into the man's side as he spun. The gun fired into the wall beside Juan. The explosion sounded like thunder in the hallway. The man lay lifeless on the dark wood floor, a puddle of blood forming under his back. Juan regretted the damage to the man's jacket, which he intended to wear as a trophy. He bent over and stripped off the jacket and a silver necklace.

Pain exploded in his left thigh, and the sound of the pistol rocked the hallway again. Juan turned to see the giant, mustachioed Mendoza coming toward him. He was also dressed in black and silver. He was so wide his shoulders almost touched the wall on each side of the hall, and his big belly caused him to lean slightly backward to maintain balance. He carried a sword in his left hand and a dueling pistol in the other. When Juan turned and raised his knife to meet the challenge, Mendoza dropped the empty pistol and shifted the sword to his right hand. A wicked smile twisted his face when he saw Juan's leg was useless.

Juan, again enraged at the sight of his enemy, tried to spring forward. When he did, the injured leg collapsed, and he fell against the wall. Mendoza charged with his sword extended. Juan raised himself to a crouch; and as Mendoza approached, top-heavy and slightly out of control, he sprang forward with his good leg, deflecting the sword with his shield and at almost the same instant taking Mendoza's legs from under him. Juan's shield clattered to the floor.

The big-bellied man tumbled down the hall like a drunk man. Unfortunately, Juan could not spring on top of him; his leg was numb. Even wounded, though, Juan was on his feet well before Mendoza struggled up. Desperately, Juan hopped forward on his good leg, dragging the other behind. Mendoza did not choose to renew the fight. Without even glancing back, he made for the door. Juan, a skilled knife thrower, knew this could be the last chance he would have to get Mendoza. Normally, he could have put the blade between Mendoza's shoulders with ease at such a short distance. Now, he had trouble keeping his balance as he threw. The knife drove into Mendoza's left shoulder, too far to the left and too high.

Mendoza wheeled around like a wounded bull. He reached over his shoulder, jerked out Juan's knife, and threw it on the floor behind him. Then he lifted his sword, "I am going to cut you into little pieces, cabron." This time he approached his wounded prey cautiously.

Juan leaned against the wall. He could neither attack nor retreat. He could only die with dignity. He bitterly regretted it would be at the hands of such a pig.

"You are a Mexican!" cried Mendoza as he neared Juan.

Juan drew himself up straight; he was several inches taller than Mendoza. "And you are not a Mexican," he countered, the Spanish words coming easily to his tongue. "You are a devil, sired by a devil and mothered by a pig. In a few minutes you will die and go to your Hell, where you will be with your brother devils." He spat down into Mendoza's face.

Mendoza laughed wickedly as he wiped the spittle from his cheek. "It is you who will be in Hell. I have killed your friends, and now I will slaughter you." He raised his sword to strike. When he did, an arrowhead popped from his chest. His eyes protruded in pain and disbelief as he dropped his sword and sank to his knees.

Juan looked over Mendoza's head. Eagle was standing in the entrance fitting another arrow to his bow. Juan held up a hand to stop him and said to Mendoza, "Now you will die in pain, you devil, as you made my father Jorge Saavedra die." Mendoza's eyes filled with fear, and he tried hard to say something as he raised his hands in supplication. Then he pitched forward and lay lifeless at Juan's feet.

"How bad is it, little brother?" called Eagle, running toward him.

Juan heaved a great sigh of relief. "It is not bad." He touched Mendoza's head and shouted, "Aiee!" Then he removed the scalp with Eagle's knife.

That evening after Talks to Horses had doctored Juan's leg, the injured warrior and his blood brother stood side by side before the campfire and gave the other warriors an exciting account of how they killed the giant pig who killed Juan's father. Then the two brothers generously dispensed the horses, jewels, and other spoils taken from the hacienda. Though Juan Horse enjoyed the glory of the moment, he enjoyed more the knowledge that finally the greatest of injustices had been punished.

THE CAPTIVE: TERESA

PART 1: HER CAPTURE

When Teresa heard the frightful screams, she cried *"Comanche!"* to her little brother, Juan. *"Adentro!"* she cried again. Juan stared in fascination. She ran over and grabbed his shoulder. *"Date prisa!"* He started running, and she grabbed little Ana, who was lying on a blanket in the sun, and ran after him.

They did not make it to the casa grande. A warrior with a red-painted face scooped up Teresa and the baby as if they were dolls and set them behind him on his pony. She could hardly stay on because of her long orange skirt. Sitting sideways and bouncing up and down, she held onto the nearly naked warrior with her left arm and her baby with the other. Her alternative was to slip off the horse and be trampled by the screaming warriors just behind.

Ahead she could see Juan on the back of a black and white paint. She looked around frantically for help. Most of the workers were out in the fields, but where were the men working in the stables? she wondered. Of course, they would be hiding somewhere. Who wanted to fight a swarm of barbarians? Her husband, Antonio, had gone to market in Chihuahua. She wished he were here to save her. No, she was glad he was away; the raiders would kill him, or worse—take him away and torture him. It was bad enough they had Ana and Juan. "Madre de Dios," she prayed, "ampárame en esta hora mala."

Two of the stable hands, Esteban and Felipe, rushed out of the stable with pitchforks. Old Esteban, who had once been a soldier, parried the lance of a warrior on a white horse and stabbed him with the pitchfork. Immediately, six others came for them. Felipe turned and ran back inside the stables. Esteban held his ground and stabbed at another of the attackers. They rode a little circle around him, almost playfully, and then two of them lanced him. One jumped off his horse, touched Esteban's body and yelled, "Aiee!"

The rider Teresa was with drew near to see the action. Riding out of the stable was a warrior holding up a dripping scalp. Another warrior was on the ground working on Esteban. Teresa looked away and swallowed back her nausea. "Madre de Dios!" she cried again and again.

Her captor turned toward the casa grande; and as they approached, she heard a woman's scream. Teresa's grandmother was alone inside, working in the kitchen. Teresa screamed in agony. Her grandmother had looked after Juan and her since their parents' deaths. Now Juan and Ana were all the family she had left. She looked around frantically for Juan. He was gone.

Teresa's right arm was almost numb from holding the baby. When she released her grip on her captor so she could try to switch arms, she started slipping from the horse. Two other warriors raced over and grabbed them. One took her, and the other wrenched little Ana away. "Mi niñita! Mi niñita!" she screamed. The warrior with Ana galloped away, holding Ana in the crook of his arm like a sack of wheat. Teresa screamed hysterically and pounded on the back of her new captor. He reached back and slapped her, almost knocking her from the horse. Bright lights danced in her eyes.

The rest of the raid on Don Sanchez's hacienda seemed interminable to Teresa, though she knew it lasted less than an hour. The raiders split into two groups. One raided the casa grande again, loading up two of Don Sanchez's burros with the plunder. The other group rounded up all the horses and burros in sight. There were not so many horses as usual, because Don Sanchez had recently sold some, and others were in use elsewhere. They found fewer than twenty.

The baby changed captors several times during the raid and so did Teresa. She panicked each time she saw the baby grabbed or tossed about.

The whole group, numbering forty or more, rode through the green valley belonging to Don Sanchez and turned north into a landscape with more hills and less vegetation. The camp was on the side of the hill. When they arrived late in the afternoon, two dozen women were packing. Teresa supposed they would move on in case there was pursuit from Mexican soldiers. She prayed there would be.

Part 2:
HER CAPTIVITY

Six or eight women, singing and yelling, ran to see the return of their husbands. They were particularly excited to see the captives and pulled Teresa from her horse. They had already torn off her blouse and skirt and were tearing at her undergarments when a tall, handsome young chief wearing a necklace of buck's teeth strode over and pushed them away. He gave some sharp orders, and they reluctantly went back to their packing. One was wearing Teresa's orange skirt. When they had quieted down, Teresa could hear Ana crying.

"Por favor, senor!" She pled with the young chief. "Mi niñita!" He looked at her uncomprehendingly. She pantomimed the act of rocking a baby in her arms. The chief nodded and summoned a younger warrior, to whom he gave instructions. In a few minutes the warrior returned with Ana, still crying. The young chief stayed by her until she had the baby nursing; then he left them alone, because the other Comanches were assembling in a circle for some kind of conference. Ana grunted contentedly as she nursed hungrily at Teresa's breast. Teresa thanked God for the handsome young chief.

She was guardedly optimistic. The chief had shown compassion, something she had not expected to receive. If she could take care of little Ana, she could bear the other indignities that were sure to come, no matter what they were. She thought of Antonio. What anguish he would feel when he came home to find his wife and baby kidnapped! She said a prayer for him. She wished she could hold him to her breast also. Panic gripped her heart as she realized she might never see him again. She tried not to think about that. Sometimes kidnapped people were bought back. Don Sanchez was a kind-hearted man.

The conference lasted about half an hour. Things apparently were not going well, because Teresa heard loud, angry voices. Carrying her sleeping baby, she walked nearer the circle. The young chief was speaking loudly and gesturing dramatically to another of the chiefs who was sitting with his back to Teresa. He was wearing a buffalo headdress. Some, but not all, of the other warriors were nodding their agreement.

When the young chief finished his speech, he stormed angrily from the circle, and fewer than half the warriors stood and followed. They quickly assembled with some of the women and prepared to leave. Teresa's heart sank when she saw Juan was being taken away, his hands tied behind his back. He looked around frantically and finally saw her. She waved at him, and he nodded back. Although she prayed fervently that the handsome young chief would come back for her, he rode away with Juan, several women, about half the Comanche warriors, and most of the horses.

As soon as the others were gone, five of the women came over and started heckling Teresa and hitting her with sticks. This did not last long, because the chief in the buffalo headdress rose and came to see about her. He ran the other women off and looked Teresa over like a man trading a horse. He liked what he saw. He admired her face, he stroked her long brown hair, and he felt her arms and legs. When Teresa recoiled at his touch, he laughed with delight. She thought she had never seen such an ugly human being. His vermillion paint did not hide a scar that started at the middle of his forehead and ran down between his evil eyes to the bottom of his right cheek.

He called a short, muscular man to his side and spoke briefly. The short man said in broken Spanish. "I White Dog. Penateka chief named Kicking Bird. You his now. He marry you soon."

"Tell him I cannot marry him. I have a husband. Please let me go home!"

White Dog interpreted. Kicking Bird laughed loudly and gave more instructions through his interpreter. "Chief say he have a wife, too. Need one more. Say his tepee your home now."

"Never! Never! Never!" Teresa was almost hysterical. Ana, disturbed by her mother's distress, began to cry.

Kicking Bird spoke angrily to White Dog. "Chief say no crying."

Teresa rocked Ana frantically and tried to speak soothingly. Ana cried even louder. Kicking Bird reached over and grabbed the baby.

"Dame mi niñita!" screamed Teresa. She tugged at Ana. Kicking Bird smothered Ana with his hand and kicked Teresa in the stomach. She fell gasping for air; her stomach had a great knot of pain. When Ana was silent, he dropped her on the ground beside Teresa. She struggled to her knees and picked up the lifeless baby, rocking her gently. After a few seconds Ana murmured slightly and began to breathe irregularly. Excitedly, Teresa rubbed her baby and spoke in her ear. Ana cried louder, and Teresa put a breast to the baby's mouth. Ana kept crying.

Kicking Bird yanked Ana from her and tossed her into a clump of cactus nearby. When Teresa tried to get up to help

Ana, Kicking Bird knocked her down again and put his foot on her back, laughing. Ana whimpered only a little and was quiet. Teresa struggled until she fainted from exhaustion.

The autumn night air was chilly, and there was a light mist. After the Penateka women had made lean-tos of buffalo skins, they lay comfortably with their husbands on blankets stolen from the casa grande. Teresa was not permitted inside Kicking Bird's lean-to, which he shared with a fat, mean-looking woman with dirty, tangled hair. Kicking Bird gave orders to White Dog. He tied Teresa's feet securely and made her lie out in the open air. "Kicking Bird say you sleep outside. Learn to be good wife." Though she was cold and uncomfortable, she was grateful not to have to sleep with Kicking Bird. The misery she felt was not from the cold or from the light rain which drenched her and mixed with her tears.

After awhile something occurred to her, and she stopped crying. Ana had already been baptized, and she was in heaven. She was free from all the horrors of captivity. Teresa thanked God for that. Her gratefulness kept her from sinking into self-pity, and she began to pray for Antonio and for Juan. She prayed Antonio would not worry about her and that they could be together again soon. She prayed Juan's life was going better than hers. Remembering the handsome young chief, she felt sure it was. And she prayed God would give her the strength to endure her present suffering. Just before daybreak the rain stopped, and she slept fitfully.

In the morning Kicking Bird's ugly, fat wife, whom he called Tasiwoo, untied Teresa and, goading her with a lance, made her fetch wood for a fire. At the bottom of the hill they had gathered some dead wood, and she had to haul up four loads on her back, protected only by her cotton slip. When she tried to ask for one of the tough buckskin shirts worn by the other women, they prodded her with the point of a lance. The wood tore holes and left splinters in her back and shoulders.

Her feet hurt worse. She had been barefoot since she was captured; and even though she often went barefoot around the hacienda, her feet were not tough enough to climb hills with big loads on her back. Her feet had some bad cuts before she finished the job. When she stumbled or went too slow, the fat woman hit her savagely with the handle of the lance.

After breakfast, which consisted of nearly raw beef that Teresa could not bear to eat, Tasiwoo, with the help of three other women, came out to cut off Teresa's hair. Though she was slender, Teresa was strong, and she struggled fiercely. The warriors came to watch but did not interfere, even when Teresa knocked Tasiwoo down with her right hand and grabbed her lance.

The other women backed away from the lance, and Teresa stood over the fat woman. As much as she wanted to, she could not kill. It was against God's law. Teresa dropped the spear and sat down. The women cut her hair off less than an inch from the scalp. After the sun burned off the early morning clouds, her scalp began to roast.

When Tasiwoo and Teresa had everything packed for the morning departure, Kicking Bird appeared with Teresa's hair braided into his. He strutted proudly before the other warriors, who nodded admiringly.

Tasiwoo and two of the other women made Teresa catch a burro to ride. It was a burro that did not want to be ridden, and it ran from Teresa, who knew almost nothing about such animals. She had ridden a horse only a few times.

When she did get a rope around its neck, the animal yanked so hard Teresa fell on her stomach and was dragged at least ten feet before it gave up. Her slip was torn and bloody when she regained her feet, and her knees were skinned badly.

One of the women held the burro's head and indicated Teresa should get on. There was no bridle and no saddle, not even a blanket. When Teresa was astraddle the burro, the woman let go, and it bucked her off. This process went on for some time with the women laughing and jeering at her. Tasiwoo was especially enjoying the struggle. If Teresa refused to climb on, the woman whipped her with a rawhide rope while the others held lances threateningly. Finally, Kicking Bird gave a command, and a woman put a bridle on the burro. Tired from its struggles, it let Teresa ride, though occasionally a woman would whack it with a stick, and it would buck her off again, to everyone's amusement.

Teresa was in terrible pain. Her body was covered with cuts and bruises from her falls, and her back was bloody from carrying the wood and from the whip of Tasiwoo. Particularly painful were some cactus thorns in her left leg. She was not permitted to stop to pull them out. Having to sit astraddle the burro without a saddle also caused her great discomfort. Her crotch and her back hurt, and she was getting blisters inside her thighs. She looked pleadingly up to the sky.

During the afternoon the warriors left with the burro and twenty horses, and Teresa was permitted to rest awhile. Though the women refused to give her food or drink, one of the younger ones let her use an awl to dig out the thorns that had broken off under the skin of her feet. She had just finished with the thorns when the warriors returned without the twenty horses. The burro was loaded with Spanish weapons, fabrics, and cheap jewelry. Teresa guessed White Dog had learned his Spanish from the traders that operated between Chihuahua and Santa Fe.

With the horses gone and her burro loaded down, Teresa had to walk. She looked ahead to the northern horizon. The land was mostly flat, the soil soft and sandy, and the trees sparse. Also there was a trail beaten down by frequent horse traffic. At least now her feet would be spared more abuse. No sooner had she thought it than the Penatekas left the trail and turned to the northeast. No one would give her moccasins. By late afternoon her feet were badly swollen from the thorns and bruises. If she ever slowed down to pull a thorn, a woman would run up behind her and hit her with a stick. Once she fell down when she was hit, and several other women ran up to join in the beating.

Well before dark the group stopped and made camp on the east side of another hill. It was a small, barren hill, from which Teresa could see all the way to the horizon. The women tried to make Teresa carry bundles of supplies up the hill, but she fainted from fatigue half way up with the first load. They let her lie there awhile and then made her join the group at the top.

She had dinner with Tasiwoo and Kicking Bird, who was nice to her. He gave her a pair of moccasins and her orange skirt. He even made Tasiwoo bring her a good supper of dried buffalo and a delicious mush containing honey and some kind of meal she did not recognize. Also she received all the water she wanted. Her spirits rose a little. The evening was balmy, her stomach was full. She would be able to sleep away some of the pain and fatigue. After dinner she lay down on a buffalo robe Kicking Bird provided. She went to sleep well before dark despite all the noises of the warriors and their singing.

Someone shook her. She looked around groggily. "Kicking Bird say you sleep with him." White Dog pointed to a lean-to nearby. She had prayed this part of the torture would never come. She had hoped she would die of disease, snakebite, or fatigue before she had to be with him. She always tried to be gentle and kind to people and pray for her enemies. She hated Kicking Bird, though. She would not even try praying for him, unless it was to pray he would burn in Hell forever, and she hoped one day to have the opportunity to send him there. White Dog yanked her to her feet and pushed her toward the ultimate indignity.

After Teresa's night with Kicking Bird, Tasiwoo was even more cruel to Teresa, cutting her rations and never letting her stop to rest. By the third day Teresa could not keep up with the group, no matter how they beat or threatened her. She had been running a fever and was so weary she could hardly put one foot in front of another. Kicking Bird made the women take turns letting her ride double with them. It was not comfortable, but it was much better than the walking. By afternoon her fever was gone and she began to think about escape. Even if they killed her, she would be better off, and she would be with Ana.

When they made camp near a grove of trees in the evening, Teresa pretended to faint from fever and exhaustion. She neither cried nor moved a muscle when Kicking Bird struck her repeatedly with a stick. Concerned he would lose a valuable possession, Kicking Bird had a lean-to built over her, and made Tasiwoo feed her milk and some kind of bread made from corn. She even put a blanket over her.

Part 3:
HER ESCAPE

During the night a thunderstorm blew in, knocking over lean-tos, putting out fires, and causing such a disturbance that the horses broke loose. Tasiwoo, who was guarding Teresa, ran to help recover them. Teresa felt God was finally helping her. The Penatekas might not even be able to follow her after the wind and rain destroyed her tracks. As soon as Tasiwoo was gone, Teresa ran.

She would let the wind blow her along for awhile until she found a hiding place. No, that would be what the Penatekas would expect. She summoned all her energy, uttered a prayer for God's help, and turned into the wind and rain, running blindly. She stumbled over brush and bumped into occasional trees, but she refused to stop, no matter how much she hurt. She even crawled awhile when she could not run anymore. Her body was a living agony. She rested awhile and struggled forward some more, crawling much of the time. When light appeared in the east, the storm abated, and she found a clump of trees to hide in. Surely, the wind and rain had destroyed her tracks. Surely, she would be safe here.

Her garments were shredded and she was shivering from fever and exhaustion. Still, she took the time to conceal herself carefully before she collapsed into the damp undergrowth.

The morning was bright, clear, and warmer. She had a fever, but she felt better because she was free for the first time in what seemed like years. She thanked God for His deliverance. While she was praying, she heard voices. Had she been running in circles all night? She thought she heard the voice of White Dog.

She clutched her hands and whispered, "Madre de Dios, ampárame en esta hora mala. Madre de Dios, ampárame en esta hora mala." The voices faded.

She lay quietly most of the day, letting the warm sun soothe her miserable body. In late afternoon she rose and stretched. She felt something she had not felt in a long time—hope. She limped through the bushes and trees. Before her was a beautiful wide river. She was sure it was the Rio Grande she had heard of all her life but never seen. She felt like the Children of Israel at the Red Sea. If only the waters would separate and she could cross over on dry land!

She realized she was getting delirious. The fever had dehydrated her body; her lips were swollen and scabbed with blood. She almost fell forward into the river as she bent down to drink and bathe herself with handfuls of water. When she felt stronger, she walked along the river and found delicious wild berries she could not identify. She hoped they were not poisonous as she ate ravenously and then lay back on the bank for a nap in the warm sun.

Voices drifted down the river. Teresa swam up from the bottom of a cold, dark pool to consciousness. She thought the Penatekas had found her again. Her body refused to move. Why should she bother?

"¿Crees que podamos pararnos aquí un momento?"

"Como no."

They were not Penatekas. Teresa jumped up and pulled the orange skirt up over her nearly naked breast. Then she ran to the top of the bank and waved wildly with her free hand at the party of about fifty soldiers and monks preparing to ford the river.

"Madre de Dios!" The shocked monks crossed themselves and ran to her side. They covered her with a robe and took her to their horses, where they gave her wine, white bread, and cheese.

After listening to a brief account of her capture and escape, they explained they were going to the mission in San Antonio. They would take her with them, and when she was strong again, she could return to Chihuahua with some of the soldiers.

Teresa wept with anguish and relief. Her baby was dead; her brother was gone, probably forever; her husband was racked with fear for her; and she had been dishonored. But God had spared her from death and from the detestable Comanche.

12

THE AMBUSH

Sitting on a brown and white mustang, he squinted his eyes and looked eastward across the parched plains. Iron Bow had never felt such heat so early in the morning. If there were not rain soon, The People would have to follow the game south toward the Stinking Buffalo River. He wondered for the first time if old Whitewater had strong enough medicine to bring rain. A week ago, after his two-day rain dance, he had predicted rain and fresh game within the week.

The second part of his prophecy at least had come true. Yesterday morning Two Hatchets' hunting party killed three antelope. That was the first game Iron Bow had seen in the past two moons. Then, in the afternoon, Red Wolf's party turned up with six freshly killed turkeys. His own party of six, led by Never Ran, had nothing. Iron Bow's stomach rumbled with hunger. For three days they had searched from morning till night, going to all the well-known and little-known hunting spots they could think of.

Before they left for the hunt, Fighting Eagle had ordered all the hunting parties to return after three days, so at sunrise this morning Never Ran reluctantly gave the order to return. He had never come back without success when he led a hunting party, or any other kind of party. He often boasted that none but Fighting Eagle had stronger medicine than he, and Iron Bow believed it was so; that was why he had joined Never Ran. This failure, however, would greatly damage his reputation.

Iron Bow and the other four hunters, all very young, looked up at the mesa, where Never Ran, riding as advance scout, was waving frantically. Iron Bow thought he must have seen buffalo to signal with such enthusiasm. They galloped up a sloping side of the mesa.

A covered wagon moved slowly along the trail below, dust blowing behind it. White men rode in front and back; they were heading toward a white man's village to the south. Never Ran said excitedly, "It will have to go through Four-Rock Pass; that is where we will ambush it."

The other warriors, including Iron Bow's brother, Hunting Horse, turned their horses to go. Iron Bow shouted, "Wait!" They looked at him impatiently. They were frustrated after the days of searching and not finding. They were hungry for action as well as for food.

"What is it?" Never Ran asked with annoyance. "We must hurry to reach the pass before the wagon!"

"Attacking that wagon would be a great mistake."

"It will be easy," said Hunting Horse, "and we will each have a horse, some food, and who knows what other wealth to take home."

"Scalps!" chimed in Stumbling Bear. He was the youngest, next to Hunting Horse, and had never taken a scalp.

"You heard Fighting Eagle say to avoid trouble with the white man. That Kiowa attack two moons ago on the wagons has brought many long-knife soldiers," countered Iron Bow.

"We have not seen any," scoffed Never Ran. "We have traveled far." He made a circle in the air with his right hand.

Iron Bow cautioned, "The wagon has at least three long knives with guns, maybe more. The deaths of three or even ten long knives would not be worth the death of one of The People."

"Is the oldest son of the great Fighting Eagle afraid?" taunted Never Ran.

"Fighting Eagle says never attack unless you have planned carefully and victory is certain," cautioned Iron Bow.

"We have our five rifles and your bow," said Never Ran. "The long knives will not hear the shots that kill them." He set his jaw in determination. "We can do it without Iron Bow."

Iron Bow looked at Hunting Horse for support. He had already pointed his sorrel toward the wagon. Iron Bow nudged the sides of his own horse. He knew this was a mistake, but he could not let his little brother go without him.

By racing at top speed, they arrived at the pass in time to conceal themselves, three on each side. The ones on the east side were to eliminate the front rider and the driver. Those on the west side were to kill the trailing rider and anyone coming out of the wagon. The task would be made difficult by gusts of wind from the south.

The wagon trail went through the middle of the pass, about three hundred feet from each side, a short distance for a good long bow under ordinary circumstances. But with the winds blowing in gusts through the pass, these were not ordinary circumstances.

Iron Bow stroked his bow. He had made it himself from buffalo horns. It had taken many hours to prepare the strips of bone and glue them together. Then he had rubbed and polished it for days before binding the joints with sinew. It was a strong bow, bigger than other warriors used. He had always been stronger and bigger in the shoulders than other warriors and, therefore, had used a bigger bow. He was also a better bowman than anyone else in the band. His father had recently changed his name from Shooting Star to Iron Bow.

With his long bow ready, Iron Bow hid with Hunting Horse and Stumbling Bear on the east side. Both had their rifles held ready to fire. They did not have to wait long. The wagon came into the pass with the two teams of horses at a full gallop; the long knife obviously was concerned about an ambush.

Iron Bow had cautioned his group to wait until the wagon was well into the pass before they fired. He felt sure Never Ran had given his group a similar warning. Unfortunately for them, however, someone in Never Ran's group fired almost as the wagon entered the pass, and it started to turn before Iron Bow had a good shot.

While Hunting Horse and Stumbling Bear were shooting wildly, Iron Bow climbed onto the rock he had been hiding behind and took careful aim at the back of the closest rider, who was riding beside the wagon. He waited an instant for the scorching wind to subside and then released the arrow. The rider fell, the arrow protruding from the middle of his back. The wagon was out of range before he could get another good shot. He turned, thinking Never Ran would give up the attack now that the ambush had failed.

Almost as the thought came into Iron Bow's mind, Never Ran and the others jumped on their horses and rode for the pass, holding their rifles high and screaming. When he looked around, he saw Hunting Horse and Stumbling Bear on their horses, headed toward the wagon. Iron Bow could not abandon his friends, even if his better judgment told him pursuit was folly.

By the time Iron Bow caught up with the others, the white rider had dropped behind the wagon, throwing his rifle on the ground in disgust and riding low on his pony. Iron Bow knew the white man hoped one or more warriors would stop to pick up the valuable rifle. He admired this long knife who was willing to risk his possessions and his life for his friends.

The man appeared to be unarmed until Never Ran and his warriors were within fifty feet. Having fired all their bullets, they were going to lance the long knife. As they raised their lances, he produced a long-barreled hand gun and fired on them, wounding Never Ran and killing his brother, White Elk.

Never Ran, despite his wound, jumped from his pony onto the white man, and the two fell to the ground. Iron Bow could not see the ensuing struggle, which resulted in the deaths of both men. He and the others were giving full attention to the wagon. It was losing speed. He soon discovered why when he saw the last of Never Ran's warriors, Big Tree, pitch from his horse. The man who had been driving was at the back of the wagon with a rifle. Someone had moved from inside the wagon to take over the reins.

"Let them go!" Iron Bow shouted. Three were already dead; there was no point in keeping at something that was foolish from the start. Either Hunting Horse and Stumbling Bear did not hear, or they ignored his command. Within a few seconds Stumbling Bear fell from his horse. The wagon was bouncing crazily, and dust must have been obscuring the white man's vision.

When Hunting Horse saw his friend fall, he dug his heels into his horse's flanks, and the mustang responded with increased speed. The white man reloaded and fired. When he bent to reload again, Hunting Horse was only a few feet from the wagon. He lunged from his horse. Catching hold of the tailgate, he struggled inside while the white man was trying to push him away. Both men disappeared from view inside the wagon.

Frantically, Iron Bow whacked his horse's rump with his bow. Just as he reached the wagon, he heard a shot and a scream. The scream was not from Hunting Horse. Iron Bow grabbed a brace on the back of the wagon and swung inside. What he saw would never pass from his memory. Hunting Horse was sitting with his back to the sideboards on the right, bouncing up and down; blood flowed from a bullet wound in his chest. The white man was bouncing face down in the front of the wagon.

Unmanly tears flooded Iron Bow's eyes as he embraced his dying brother. Then he held him by the shoulders and said, "I will get you back to your tepee, Little Brother."

Hunting Horse smiled faintly and nodded toward the white man. Iron Bow understood. "Yes, he is dead."

Hunting Horse smiled again, and his mouth moved soundlessly as he slumped in death. Iron Bow was filled with both grief and a sense of anguished futility. To die courageously was the hope of all warriors. Hunting Horse had done that, but the cause was foolish.

Iron Bow gently laid his brother on the floor of the bouncing wagon. As he did so, he sensed a movement behind him. It was careless of him to assume the fallen white man was dead. He spun around in time to take a knife in his upper arm. Though the man's force was weak, the knife was sharp and cut deep. Iron Bow had whipped out his own knife as he turned. He plunged it into the white man's chest. He withdrew it quickly and crawled to the front. One more long knife must die.

The driver looked back when Iron Bow pulled the curtain that had closed off the front of the wagon. Her large blue eyes filled with horror at the sight of the half-naked warrior, and she began to scream hysterically.

Iron Bow sprang to her side, hoping to grab the reins, but she had already lost them, and the wagon was bouncing wildly away from the wagon trail. He jumped onto the backs of the near team and struggled along the wagon tongue to the lead team. His left arm was afire with pain, and his eyes and nose were clogged by the billowing dust.

His pain and effort proved futile. Before he could stop the horses, the wagon hit a giant ditch. The sudden jerk pulled the horses to the ground and sent Iron Bow into a sprawl.

After lying disoriented in the dirt a few minutes, he stood shakily like a dog that a bear had mauled. The wagon was in pieces, its canopy torn into dirty brown ribbons and its wheels broken and scattered. Only two bodies were near the wreckage. He looked around. It was easy to see the white woman's golden hair, even though she had hidden in a scraggly patch of bushes a hundred paces away.

He turned and walked slowly back to the wreckage, where he found Owl's Call, the big sorrel Talks to Horses had given Hunting Horse two winters ago when he first took the warrior's road. After carefully extricating his brother's body from the wreckage, Iron Bow tied it to the back of the sorrel and then whistled for his mustang, Storm.

When he had rounded up the other four horses and secured the body of each warrior to his respective mount, it was past midafternoon, and he was weakened from the oppressive heat and from his wound, which he had bound awkwardly with a square of white cotton cloth he found in the wreckage. The rag was soaked with blood, which also ran down his arm and dripped from his elbow. Through all his labored activity he kept an eye on the woman, who had hardly moved. She was clever.

He considered leaving her. Collecting her would take time, and in his present state of grief and physical pain, he wanted to return to his village as quickly as possible. Also, he was weakening noticeably. He did not want to lose consciousness out here. Some predator, perhaps even the woman, might kill him in the night. But if he left her here alone, she would almost certainly die. She was like a little bird fallen from a nest.

The only water within miles was what he carried in his water bag; the water barrel on the wagon had broken in the crash. He was pretty sure she had no weapon, and he had collected all those of the dead men. Perhaps, he would leave her a rifle to protect herself from predators. If she made it through the night, she could find her way to the white man's village. He would have to leave her water, too, and a horse. He did not like the idea of giving up a rifle and a horse that would be compensation for the family of a dead warrior. Besides, he doubted she knew enough to find the white man's village. She would probably wander around aimlessly and finally die anyway.

He knew she would be starving for water, when he mounted Storm and waved for her to surrender. Seeing him coming for her, she ran desperately toward the hills, but she was too weak and thirsty to run fast. He slid from his horse and grabbed her. She flailed her arms wildly, battering his injured arm and pulling free. He grabbed again and ended up with nothing but an empty sleeve.

Iron Bow was in no mood for a struggle with this wildcat, who looked like she was ready to fight to the death. He kicked her feet from under her and whipped out his knife ready to solve the problem of what to do with her. Defenseless, she lay before him.

He could not kill her. Something inexplicable made him hold back the blade that he would thrust into her heaving breast. It was not the fear in her eyes. He had often slit the throats of rabbits and deer with that same look. There was something about her that would not permit her being killed.

When he withdrew the knife, their eyes locked in speechless conversation for what seemed like a long time. Then he put his knife back into its sheath and handed her his water bag. She looked puzzled and would not take the water. He knelt beside her and put the water to his mouth and drank. "It is good water," he assured her in his language and offered the bag to her again. She touched his hand with hers as she held the bag to her cracked and bleeding lips. Some of it ran down her chin as she drank thirstily between gasps for breath. She never took her eyes from his.

"What are you going to do with me?" She saw he did not understand her words and tried again, "Are you going to kill me?" She pointed to his knife.

He shook his head. He was moved by her beauty and her vulnerability. He had no love for the long knife; he was an invader, threatening to destroy The Comanche's hunting grounds. Iron Bow had no more qualms about killing her friends than if they had been wild dogs attacking his horses. He felt compassion for her, though.

Feeling weak, he sat on the ground cross-legged and made her sit in front of him. Speaking softly and using sign language, he thought she might understand, he told her of the condition of his band, the reason for the day's hunt and how he had opposed the unfortunate attack on the wagon. He told of his intentions to take her back to his village and assured her she would not be killed.

Iron Bow could see she did not understand what he was saying, but she appeared to be comforted by his tone of voice. When he stood and pointed to the white man's horse he had caught for her to ride, she immediately mounted, having to pull her long dress up so she could sit on the saddle correctly. Her legs were long and as white as a summer cloud. Her brown shoes covered her ankles. Even though she appeared to be about his age, he was surprised by her agility.

She pulled her dress down to cover as much of her legs as possible and turned to look at the five Indian ponies with their sad loads. "All your friends are dead." Her voice was tender and sad. "And all my friends are dead." She looked at him. "Why?" She wiped her eyes with the back of her arm.

He sensed the meaning of the question; it was uppermost in his own mind, and he wished he had the words to answer it for her. Instead of answers he had anger and sorrow. The anger was partly for his own foolish companions but mostly for the white man. And in a way it was right to blame the white man, because the land had belonged to The People for as long as anyone could remember.

The white man was the invader, the thief. He was claiming big pieces of land and killing buffalo. He killed it only for the hide and left the meat to rot. Last fall Iron Bow had seen a thousand carcasses rotting in the sun, and he had wept for the great animals and for The People, who would starve if the white man killed all the buffalo. In the winter a long-knife chief talked to his father and promised to live peacefully with The People and respect his hunting grounds, but Fighting Eagle said the long knife could not be trusted.

Iron Bow looked out across the prairie for signs of other human life. He heard only the quietness he loved, now broken by the steps of the horses and the rattling sounds of the cicada. The sky was a deep blue, accented by occasional wisps of white clouds. The sun seemed hotter than he had ever felt it. He wiped perspiration from his forehead as he shifted on his pony to search the horizon behind. There was nothing but scattered trees and brown grass between him and the distant hills.

He looked at the woman. Her eyes, though red and swollen from crying, were beautiful. They were the color of the blue morning flower he once found near the banks of the Arrowhead River. And her face had the elegance of that same flower. It was slender and only lightly tanned, framed by curls as yellow as the gold he had brought back from his first raid below the Stinking Buffalo River. When the wind shifted, he smelled a flower fragrance from her. He was struck by the fact that she was different in nearly every way from the Antelope women. Her total effect was one of delicacy, like the tracing of frost on a ripe persimmon in late autumn.

The Antelope women were harder from doing much work, and they were capable of harshness, especially toward cowardly warriors or prisoners. However, some women, in spite of the difficulties of their way of life, retained a certain enduring softness which was superior to the delicacy of this white woman. Sunny Sky had it. He thought the softness was somehow connected with their continually having to face the death of persons they loved.

He thought of Sunny Sky, whom he would soon make his wife. Her arms and legs were muscular from hours of work, and once when the village was attacked, she had killed a Kiowa with a knife. But she was gentle and loving in a way this white woman could never be. Sunny Sky knew what it was to be alive and free in the wilderness and still be a woman.

He felt pity for this white woman; she was like the little wobbly-legged fawn he found last spring after killing the mother. It had no protectors and could never be happy living in the Antelope village. He had hated to kill the small animal, even though he knew it was the merciful thing to do.

He looked at the white woman, knowing it would probably be more merciful to kill her than to take her back with the five dead bodies, which he did not have the strength to bury. The mothers and sisters would want to torture her to death. He did not think his father would want that, but sometimes he had to give in to the will of his people, just as Iron Bow had done awhile ago.

Her best protection would be for him to take her for his wife, something he did not want to do. Perhaps if he had several wives he would do it, but he wanted Sunny Sky to be his first wife, maybe his only wife ever.

The cloth around his arm was soaked and oozing. He stopped to adjust it, swinging down from his pony. The woman was quickly at his side. "Let me help you. She held his arm firmly when he tried to pull it away. "It's a nasty wound," she said as she examined it carefully. "It needs some stitches." She tore pieces of cloth from the bottom of her already ragged dress. Using the cleanest piece and some water from the bag, she cleaned the wound and poured water over it. Then with two more strips and a folded pad she put on a tight bandage that stopped the blood from oozing. Though the pain was sharp, Iron Bow stood stoically through her ministrations. He was even stirred by her closeness and her tenderness. Her breath had a sweetness to it.

He walked back to the horses laden with the warriors' bodies. He stroked the head of his little brother, who only this morning had been full of life and energy. Iron Bow slapped the sorrel's rump, and it started toward the village. All horses trained by Talks to Horses returned to the village when abandoned. The others followed, eager to get back to food and water.

Iron Bow regretted Moonflower's and Little Robin's grief when the horses returned with the dead warriors. They would think he was dead, too. And he knew his father's pain would be even greater. He had trained his sons to be superb warriors and was preparing them to be great leaders. He hoped some day to live on in them after he died. Iron Bow wondered if he should reconsider? No, he felt he must hold to his decision.

Lights flashed through his head when he swung back onto Storm; and for the first time in his life, he had doubts about his ability to accomplish a goal. Like his father he was tall and muscular and normally had great endurance. Once, when he was scouting, his horse was shot by an Apache patrol, and he ran twelve miles back to the village to warn his father. Now he was not sure; he was beginning to shiver despite the heat. Motioning to the girl to mount, he turned his horse's head toward the white man's village. He would take her close enough to find her way alone; then he would return to his village. The main thing was to remain conscious.

"I'll kill the first mother's son that lays a hand on that Indian!" The fierceness of the words brought Iron Bow back to consciousness. He thought they were directed at him. His last memory was the struggle to stay on his horse. Now it was morning, and he was lying on a soft bed in a white man's tepee. His arm hurt still; otherwise he felt good. Beside him, looking worried, was the blue-eyed girl. At the foot of the bed stood a tall, bearded white man dressed in buckskin. He was pointing a rifle at three other white men standing near the door. Two were blue-shirted soldiers with pistols pointed at Iron Bow.

"He brought Elizabeth to me, and for that he leaves alive—unharmed!"

"Aw, come on, Baxter," said the man beside the soldiers. He looked like the man in the back of the wagon, except he had red hair. "He killed white people. He maybe killed my brother."

Elizabeth asserted, "I didn't see him kill anybody. I did see him save my life."

The bearded man gestured with the rifle. "So he ain't going to die. I promised Elizabeth that. You want to kill him, you got to kill me first; and I die hard."

"I never thought I'd see you protecting an Injun devil after one of 'em killed your brother," said the red-haired man.

"Killing this one won't bring him back. This Comanche risked his neck to save Elizabeth. He could have taken her to his village, and God knows what would have become of her." He looked at Elizabeth to reaffirm his position. "He ain't going to die."

The older of the two soldiers said, "Well, if the lady won't testify against him, we sure can't hold him. Come on, sergeant. You, too, Reynolds." They left.

The man and the woman rode with him through the village of about twenty log tepees with white people, mostly women and children, standing at the doors shouting angry words. The riders looked straight ahead and said nothing.

Just outside the village, the bearded man said, "He'll be safe now, Elizabeth."

They all stopped. Iron Bow and the woman searched each other's eyes a long time before he turned Storm's head to the west.

As the horse began to gallop, Iron Bow looked at the familiar line of hills he would soon be crossing and drew a deep breath. For the first time he was aware that the weather was cooler and the ground was wet. It had rained in the night.

13

DEATH OF A SMALL WARRIOR

Iron Bow kicked his favorite roan into a gallop. The sad feeling in his heart was colder than the crisp autumn air. His son, Fighting Heart, held to his waist, his hands frail like an old woman's; the black paint on them could not disguise that.

It would be better if Fighting Heart could have ridden by himself into this, his first battle, and Iron Bow had tried tying him to a gentle mare, but the only way he could stay on was to be tied across her like a dead man. A warrior should not go into battle that way. Besides, Iron Bow liked the symbolism of riding double; at war dances it was the way warriors rode to signify they had rescued a fallen comrade in battle. Iron Bow was rescuing his son from death by illness.

Because this was their last time to ride together, they had a special feeling of closeness. And something else. Iron Bow felt medicine coming from Fighting Heart into him, and that surprised him. He had believed his own medicine would strengthen the boy to carry through this final coup. That he was receiving power from the boy reinforced his awareness that Fighting Heart was unique.

He thought back to the boy's birth. Sunny Sky was not so big as she had been with the other children, and the baby was small boned and pale in color, pale as the sun when it was obscured by a dust storm on the plains. When he cried, his whimpering was faint like the runt in a bitch's litter. Ironically, the name Fighting Eagle chose for him was Wolf Call. Throws Stones, the medicine man, urged Iron Bow to leave the baby on a mountain to die. When he told Sunny Sky, she cried and begged him not to.

It is a hard thing to kill a son. Iron Bow went to his tepee, where he smoked and prayed for hours; finally he received a vision showing him that he should let the baby live. He sent word the boy was to be called Fighting Heart.

He never regretted the decision. Even though the child was always smaller than the other children, he had great vitality and was smarter than children twice his age. When he was three, he could converse like a child of six or seven. When he was six, he remembered everything he heard or saw. He could retell without a mistake lengthy stories or repeat all the coups he had heard counted at a War Dance.

By the time he had seen nine winters, warriors would come from other bands to hear the boy repeat tales he had heard. He could present two versions, the one he had heard or the one he had embellished. His version was always superior to the original. No one had ever witnessed such intelligence in a child, and all marvelled at what he would one day be able to accomplish.

His powers were not limited to stories. He could remember hundreds of names and could store maps in his head, whether he had seen the countryside or heard it described. He knew the whole of Comanche country as well as the lands they raided. He also knew the names of all the bands around them—friendly or unfriendly—the names of their chiefs, where and when they had raided and what the results of the raids were.

Every kind of important information was passed on to him. He knew all the hunting grounds, as well as the migration habits of the wildlife The People hunted. He could make accurate predictions of where and when buffalo herds could be found. He was nearly always asked to be present when any kind of raiding or hunting party made plans.

It was after his twelfth summer that Fighting Heart sought the vision that would prepare him to ride the warrior's road. Iron Bow reflected on the episode with remorse. Even though Fighting Heart was an exceptional rider and good with weapons, he had a weak chest, frequently coughing and wiping his nose. Iron Bow had reluctantly permitted the boy to seek his vision in late fall under the supervision of Wrestled a Bear, then the most highly-respected medicine man.

On a clear crisp day like this one, Fighting Heart went to The Porcupine, a nearby mountain. The first night a freezing rain storm hit and nearly froze him to death, even though he had made a lean-to and covered himself with a buffalo robe. He came staggering down the next day with feverish tales of magnificent visions—visions like no one had ever seen before. Unfortunately, he contracted a terrible cough and ran a high fever for several days. Wrestled a Bear and two other men with strong medicine came to his tepee and tried their remedies to no avail. Then Iron Bow ordered everyone out, and he personally stayed by the boy's side, feeding him broth from boiled buffalo and constantly offering up songs and prayers at his side.

Fighting Heart's mind and soul were not harmed, but his body was. His arms were almost paralyzed. He ate rarely, and when he did eat, the portions were small, hardly enough to keep a rabbit alive. If he ate much at a time, he would vomit it. So he became thinner than a winter coyote. While he continued to receive visions of power, the power was in his spirit, not his body. If his body were as strong as his spirit, he would be the mightiest of all warriors.

That storm was the beginning of an unusually harsh winter. There had been no fall; green leaves fell from the trees under the weight of early snow. Even so, the band found plenty of game, especially deer. The bad part of the winter was that Fighting Heart was seldom able to go outside and sit or lie in the sun. If he tried, he would begin to shake with a chill, no matter how many buffalo robes he was covered with. Nothing could keep the cold air from going into his body. Father Sun could not, therefore, heal the small warrior.

With the last full moon Fighting Heart's condition worsened dramatically. He was often delirious, and the chills would not stop. Autumn Song, the beautiful daughter of Wrestled a Bear, came in to sing to him and lie in his bed with him. She was older by four winters than Fighting Heart, and her body was that of a woman. Iron Bow could see that Fighting Heart delighted in her companionship, though he barely had the strength to hold her hand.

At first, Autumn Song clearly did not wish to be with Fighting Heart, because she knew two strong, young warriors who wanted to marry her. Wrestled a Bear had made her come to him. It was his final effort to atone for his bad judgment in sending one of the Antelope's greatest assets to what was turning out to be his death. After she had spent a day at Fighting Heart's side, her attitude changed. He was weak in body only, and with her at his side the chills stopped so he could talk with her. He had a deep, manly voice, and he told her tales and visions that would enthrall even an oak tree.

Autumn Song was soon aware she was in the presence of a warrior such as the band had never seen before and would probably never see again. Her heart was won, and she was constantly at his side, feeding and caring for him in every way.

A few days after Autumn Song moved into Fighting Heart's tepee, he was in some ways stronger. He could sit up and carry on a lengthy conversation, and he could even stand outside in the sun for short periods of time, but his cough was getting worse, and the look of death was on him. Iron Bow had seen the look too many times to mistake it.

He did not want his son to die of sickness, especially when he had never been proved in battle. The Great Spirit could take no joy in such a warrior—less than a warrior—so he would not get a new body and hunt in the Great Spirit's hunting grounds. Iron Bow was deeply distressed by the prospect.

The solution came to him during a hunting trip. He and eight braves were hunting near the River of Fishes when they surprised an Apache hunting party. They were spearing fish and had not set a guard. The leader of the party was the first to hear the Antelope, and he grabbed a rifle and jumped behind a rock. The others ran for their horses and escaped while the leader covered their retreat. When he ran out of bullets, the Apache stood on the rock he had used for cover and defied the Antelope to take him. Iron Bow admired the young warrior's courage, and he told the Apache the two of them would fight; if the Apache won, he could return to his village.

The Apache, whose name was Red Sleeves, was a fierce fighter and gave Iron Bow a good struggle. He was big and strong but quick as a wildcat. He was also an excellent knife fighter, just the kind of opponent Iron Bow loved to fight. The risks must be high if one is to enjoy a thrilling victory.

Red Sleeves' abilities could not compensate for a lack of experience. Consequently, Iron Bow disarmed him at once and could have killed him. Instead, he wrestled with him for much of the afternoon. The fight ended when the Apache collapsed with exhaustion. As Iron Bow led his captive home, he was forming a plan; and on arrival at the village he would not let the women torture Red Sleeves but took him to Fighting Heart's tepee, where he presented his battle plan to the two warriors.

Sometimes a bond develops between men who have fought each other in mortal combat. Each has witnessed the other's courage and felt his strength. They have been to the door of death together, and they know each other as intimately as it is possible for one man to know another. Iron Bow had spared the life of Red Sleeves, because the Apache was exceptional in ways a warrior should be. He had fought the Apache as he might fight a wild mustang. One could not help but admire the fire and beauty of the mustang, and certainly, one did not kill him.

Using Wolf's Friend as an interpreter, Iron Bow made Red Sleeves understand his battle plan. It was clear Red Sleeves also respected Iron Bow, and he readily agreed to his part in the plan. That was two days ago.

The site of this day's battle was at the base of The Porcupine, so called because of the many sharp rocks that protruded from its surface. It was not a high mountain, but its jagged terrain made it difficult, even dangerous, to climb. It was, therefore, a favorite of young warriors. The area around the base was flat and covered with buffalo grass; there were a few scattered mesquite trees and occasional large rocks that must have rolled down the mountain. Fighting Heart had selected this spot because it was here he received his vision. If his life must end so soon, he wanted it to be at the spot where power had come into his life.

Almost everything now depended on the Apache, a bad position for a Comanche to be in, and Iron Bow looked anxiously toward the mountain still over five miles away. Two factors made Iron Bow expect the Apache to be there. The Apache had given his sacred word, and he would not want to dishonor himself. He knew also that Iron Bow would lead a vengeance raid against the Apache if Red Sleeves did not keep his word. Red Sleeves would fear for his people even if he were indifferent to his own death.

Iron Bow was relieved to see a puff of smoke rise from the top of the Porcupine. It was the signal that Red Sleeves saw them and was about to begin. Iron Bow announced, "Red Sleeves is ready."

"And Fighting Heart is ready."

Iron Bow rode to one of the larger mesquite trees and helped his son dismount. Red Sleeves would already be at the base of the mountain on the other side and ready to start his attack.

Iron Bow leaned Fighting Heart against the tree and helped him off with his buckskin shirt. "This is where you must fight, my son." He put his hand on the boy's shoulder and looked down into his eyes. He had covered his face with black and then painted yellow stripes downward from his eyes. His face looked like skin stretched across a fleshless skull, but the eyes were bright with excitement.

He struggled to hold himself erect. "No one will have cause to be ashamed of Fighting Heart." He bent over and laboriously removed his moccasins as a sign that he would hold his ground till death.

Deeply moved, Iron Bow embraced his son as he heard approaching hoofbeats; then he concealed himself and his horse behind a nearby boulder. He felt an odd mixture of dread and excitement, pain and joy, sorrow and pride.

Red Sleeves broke into the open, holding his rifle high and screaming a cry of attack. When he was within range, he began to fire his rifle into the air. He was a handsome warrior with big shoulders and chest. He wore buckskin pants, a red shirt, a buckskin vest, and a red cloth around the top of his head. He rode a brown mustang Iron Bow had given him for the occasion.

Fighting Heart stood erect on frail legs, over which his breech-cloth drooped like a buffalo robe hung on poles to dry. Despite the chill of the autumn morning, he was not shivering, and he managed to keep his head and shoulders high. He held his rifle, a lever-action Winchester, at his waist and fired in Red Sleeves' direction. Iron Bow had feared his son would not have the strength to work the lever and remain upright as well. It was important to die standing with his face to the enemy.

At Fighting Heart's second shot Red Sleeves fell from his horse as though wounded. When he did not get back up, Fighting Heart claimed this for his first kill, and yelled, "Aiee!" loudly and strongly. Red Sleeves lay still for a moment more and then jumped to his feet and remounted his horse, which was standing nearby grazing on the buffalo grass. He kicked at the horse's flanks and came galloping toward Fighting Heart.

When he was within one hundred feet, he began to circle the small warrior. As Fighting Heart fired his last shot, Red Sleeves again fell from his horse as though dead. This time Fighting Heart was only able to say, "Aiee!" softly. He was running out of strength. Heavy perspiration was flowing from his face, and his legs were trembling. Iron Bow wanted to go to his son's aid but resisted. Fighting Heart must do this alone.

Red Sleeves rose cautiously to his feet, leaving his rifle lying on the ground. He drew his knife and began a careful approach, as though he were stalking a mighty warrior. Seeing the face of his enemy, Fighting Heart seemed to gain new energy. He let his rifle drop and drew his own knife, a fine long-bladed steel knife Iron Bow had taken from a long-knife soldier. He held it in the ready position as Red Sleeves began to circle him menacingly.

Iron Bow wanted to urge Red Sleeves along. Then he remembered the Apache could see the small warrior's eyes. He would be able to know better than Iron Bow how much strength remained. Red Sleeves was a superb actor and was stretching the performance as far as it would go. When he was within two paces of Fighting Heart, he stopped short, holding his knife above his head.

Fighting Heart was so much smaller than the Apache that Iron Bow was reminded of a mountain lion stalking a rabbit. Fighting Heart did not behave as a rabbit. He straightened his shoulders and held his own knife in the striking position. He almost fell forward with the effort but quickly regained his feet and set them at shoulder width.

Red Sleeves lunged forward and drove his blade into the small warrior's chest, screaming as the knife bit into the flesh. Fighting Heart fell against Red Sleeves as the Apache withdrew his knife. He stepped backward and let the body sink to the ground face to the sky. Then he bent over Fighting Heart as though to take his scalp.

Iron Bow fired a shot that kicked up dirt beside the Apache. He jumped up and ran for his horse. Iron Bow let him mount and ride a few hundred feet before firing at him. The Apache fell from his horse and lay still for a few moments. Then he jumped back on his horse, waved at Iron Bow, and rode west.

Iron Bow returned to his fallen son. He was so small and frail that Iron Bow lifted him easily. The small warrior's blood smeared across his father's body. On his gaunt little face was a look of rapture.

THE GRAND COUP

PART 1:
GETTING READY

Over the years Iron Bow had migrated a number of times with the Antelope band. Usually they had moved to be near better hunting grounds, sometimes to avoid an unprofitable war. In recent times they were moving to avoid the white man, who could not be satisfied. When the Comanche was much stronger than the white man, he made agreements to permit the white man to own land and hunting space in what he called Tejas. Gradually more and more white men came; the agreements were broken, and the Antelope was having to move farther west into more arid country, where the climate was unpleasant and the game less plentiful.

During the present migration his people had run out of food and had decided to raid a long-knife village. Iron Bow had counseled against the raid, principally because they were traveling with women and children. He was no longer concerned with treaties; they meant nothing to the white man. But if pursuit were immediate, they would not be able to escape a battle in which they would be at a great disadvantage.

Logic is weak with starving people. They had fed on roots, grass, and insects; once he had discovered two children eating the rotting flesh of a coyote. The memory renewed the pain and hatred he felt. He turned his black horse and examined the eastern horizon. Having seen fifty winters, he was an old man to be a warrior; but his vision was still sharp. He was the first to see the small cloud of dust, and he called to two other chiefs.

He inhaled deeply. The summer morning air was fresh and good. The long knife would probably claim that, too, he thought bitterly. For years he had hoped the white man would be willing to share the land and respect it and the game that lived on it. Eventually, it became clear he intended to take everything. What he did not take he would kill or defile. More and more kept coming. These people tore at the land, built forts, and slaughtered game. Once he had seen a string of skinned buffalo carcasses that stretched as far as he could see. That was the day he began to fear his people were doomed.

Not long afterward he talked with a white man named Big Mike, who had moved to Tejas and married a Kiowa woman. He told Iron Bow of the white man's ways in war. He had a long history of wars; some were on a great scale, and he could sustain them for years. Also, Big Mike, who once lived far north of the River Colored by Clay and had seen white men as numerous as the stars, said they could not be stopped or trusted. Iron Bow knew long ago they could not be trusted. Fighting Eagle had discovered that. Now he also knew they could not be stopped.

The white man would never be content until he had destroyed The People or confined them to what he called a "reservation." Iron Bow spat into the dust beside him. He knew enough about the white man to know what a "reservation" would be like. The land area would be small, the game would be inadequate, and the inhabitants would not be free to seek new hunting grounds. He would not live that way. He would die first.

The riders causing the dust trail were his own scouts. As they approached, Iron Bow was joined by two other chiefs. One was his son Jumping Bear; the other was Angry Wolf. Jumping Bear was the most respected chief of the Antelope band next to Iron Bow.

The scouts' horses were winded and sweating heavily. "Long-knife soldiers!" shouted the lead rider. "They are tracking the Antelope!"

"How many?" asked Iron Bow.

"Maybe a hundred and fifty."

"We have two times that many warriors," said Angry Wolf. "We will ambush them."

Jumping Bear shook his head. "No, we do not have enough rifles and bullets. We must send half the warriors to attack the long knife and divert him. The others can escape during the fighting."

Iron Bow warned. "If the Antelope sends out one hundred warriors, the long knife will send three hundred soldiers for revenge. No, the Antelope cannot go to war with the long knife." He turned to the scouts. "Describe the army."

"Six wagons. The long-knife soldier was dirty and tired." This information came from the younger rider. He was Laughing Coyote, Jumping Bear's son. "Laughing Coyote waited behind a rock and watched as the long knife rode by."

Iron Bow studied the horizon a few moments and then turned to the chiefs. "If these soldiers came from the Fort-by-the-Lake to capture the Antelope, they would be clean and not tired. They have been on another journey and were sent to find us before they could rest. They will not follow the Antelope far. If we ride all through the day and the night, we will be safe." He turned back to the scouts. "How fast do they ride?"

"Their speed is twice that of the Antelope," warned Laughing Coyote.

"And it is only noon," added Angry Wolf.

Iron Bow looked across the plains, thinking about his alternatives. A plan formed itself in his mind; and he studied it, thinking of the advantages to his people. Then he turned back to the chiefs. "One man can delay them if he is clever."

Jumping Bear knew his father referred to himself. "That would be self-murder!"

"Not self-murder. A grand coup. Iron Bow is old, his wives are dead. This will be his last gift to The People."

"Laughing Coyote will go also," said the young warrior.

Iron Bow's pride showed in his smile to his grandson. "No, the hope for the Antelope lies with the young." He looked at the other chiefs. "You have families to take care of; Iron Bow is not needed as you are. Does anyone doubt his abilities?"

The other chiefs read the resolution in Iron Bow's eyes and were moved by his courage. They had sat at war councils with him and had fought beside him in wars. If there was one man who could detain the cavalry, it was Iron Bow. His strength was legendary. Once, he lifted a giant buffalo that had fallen on the legs of another warrior. Later it took three braves to lift the same buffalo. The chiefs knew he had not weakened much with age, because he still wrestled with the young warriors. None of them could defeat him.

Jumping Bear examined his father's face for signs of weakness. Iron Bow showed none. Though the skin was wrinkled and leathery now, the jaw was still firm. Like the younger warriors he wore only a breech-cloth. Unlike other older men, his body was still erect, and the skin was smooth over bulging muscles that could unleash a blow as quick as the strike of a snake.

Jumping Bear rode to Iron Bow's side, and the two chiefs looked long and affectionately into each other's eyes. Iron Bow extended his rifle, a fine repeating Winchester. "Jumping Bear will need this." Iron Bow held up his hand to silence the argument his son was about to make. "This is all Iron Bow needs." He patted the bow strung across his body. Then he rode to Laughing Coyote and handed his lance to the younger warrior.

Laughing Coyote did not argue, though it was clear he wanted to. Instead, he handed the older warrior his own quiver of arrows to supplement Iron Bow's personal supply.

He took them solemnly and then looked back at the Antelope band strung out behind him. A few children were running in play, but most of the women stood silently beside their bundles and horses. The men were all mounted and motionless, awaiting orders. He lifted his arm in farewell and turned his horse toward the morning sun. As he galloped away, the image of his son and his grandson comforted him. He wished he could have spoken to every member of the band, especially the other chiefs and the old warriors he had fought beside, but there was no time.

Part 2: THE BATTLE

After more than an hour of hard riding, Iron Bow sat on a hill that sloped down to the Talking Water River. From a small pouch of buffalo hide he took some dried beef stolen the day before from the long knife. As he chewed it slowly, savoring it, he was struck by how keen a man's senses are when he knows he will die soon. He liked the feel of the hot sun burning down on the back of his neck so much that he took off the sun shade that hung from the strips of leather around his neck. He regretted that he would never feel the cooling rain again.

He was glad his final encounter was to be at the river, a place where one could feel the presence of the Great Spirit. The river was swift and as blue as the cloudless sky; an occasional fish jumped from the water, and birds flew along the banks chasing insects. Across the river he saw a giant cottonwood in which several mockingbirds were chattering. Before the beauty was shattered by the cavalry, he would take time for songs and prayers. He needed to make strong medicine for a grand coup.

He heard the sounds of the soldiers long before he saw the first riders. For his ambush he hid behind a large rock formation at the top of the slope, which was perhaps two hundred feet from the river. It was another hundred feet or so to the middle—not a bad distance for his great bow. This was the most narrow and most shallow crossing along the river, the place the long-knife soldier was sure to use, especially since the Antelope had used it earlier.

As the blue-shirted soldiers galloped up to the river, Iron Bow heard shouts in the long-knife's language, and he heard some Antelope words, too. These words assured the long knife that all was clear. Soon, many voices carried clearly across the river, and Iron Bow heard loud splashing as the horses plunged into the water.

He knew he could kill more of the long-knife soldiers if he waited until they were in the middle of the river. The distance would be more favorable for his bow, and the soldiers would be more vulnerable in the deeper water; however, his primary object was to delay them. If he waited until they were half way, they might continue across.

He wanted to peek over his rock almost as soon as they were in the water. This was where the patience that comes from experience was valuable. He had known many ambushes to be ruined by an overeager warrior. Because so much was at stake here, he forced himself to wait a little longer than he felt was necessary.

When he stood up, some of the soldiers were nearing the middle of the river on their swimming horses, which were struggling against the swift current. His first three arrows knocked three soldiers from their horses and started a burst of shouting.

He ducked his head and ran to another rock formation to his right, not because the rifle fire was close but because he hoped to give the impression there was more than one warrior behind the rocks. Again he sent three arrows into the river, not aiming carefully now that bullets were ricocheting off the rocks around him. Two horses began to thrash violently from arrows in their necks. Another soldier floated face down. He was the one who had carried a flag with a sign on it.

Concealed from the soldiers' view, Iron Bow crawled quickly to another rock and shot several more arrows; the soldiers had turned back to the far bank. Some of the horses were climbing out of the water.

He took more careful aim now that they had stopped firing and he put arrows into four more soldiers and two horses. Then he crawled to another vantage point. Soldiers were standing on the bank firing volleys of shots at his previous positions. He jumped up and took one more good shot, hitting a soldier who was swimming without his horse. Then Iron Bow screamed as though he were shot and fell backwards behind a rock. In a crouch he ran to a patch of brush nearby where he could watch the soldiers unobserved.

They retired several hundred paces from the bank and had a conference. Iron Bow had picked out the chief, whom he could see agitatedly talking to his scout. He guessed the chief wanted to know how many Antelope warriors were across the river before he committed his men to another crossing.

That the conference lasted a good while pleased Iron Bow. The chief was confused and indecisive. His orders were vague, perhaps, having come hastily at a time when the soldier was looking forward to a good rest and good food. After talking to the scouts, he summoned two more long knives and talked with them briefly and with less gesturing. His decision was made.

First, the chief required the others to hide among the trees and rocks; then with a white cloth tied to a stick he, another long-knife soldier, and the scout rode into the water. Iron Bow could not be more pleased; talk and time could save his people. After they were out of the water, he let them stand around awhile, calling out impatiently. He did not want his stalling to become obvious, though; and he did not want the scout to advance far from the river and discover there was only one enemy.

When the scout, whom Iron Bow recognized to be Yellow Dog, dismounted and began to look for signs, Iron Bow mounted and rode into view. After fifty feet he turned and held his hands up to the hills as though he were signaling other warriors to hold their fire. He then advanced slowly and solemnly to meet the long-knife chief.

He was a slender, long-faced man with short brown hair that barely showed beneath his wide-brimmed hat.. His face was pock-marked. "I am Captain Thomas of the United States Cavalry. This is Sergeant Quinn. Your unprovoked attack will have serious consequences, unless you surrender along with the twenty-five braves who raided the Allantown settlement yesterday."

Although Iron Bow understood most of the Captain's words, he pretended ignorance. He spoke to the scout in the Antelope language, being careful to control his voice, "Does Yellow Dog now live by betraying his people? Did Iron Bow not know him as a young warrior when he swore death to all long knives?"

Yellow Dog's countenance was mixed with shame and pride. "The time is here when all who cannot fight with the white man will die on his reservation. As the white man's scout Yellow Dog can still do the things he knows best."

Iron Bow smiled so that his face would not reveal to the captain his disgust. "Yes. Drink the long knife's whiskey." He turned his head to the hills behind him. "And betray his brothers."

Captain Thomas interrupted what would appear to him a friendly exchange between old friends and talked in a whisper at length with Yellow Dog, who nodded his approval. "The Captain says Iron Bow must surrender all the warriors who raided the settlement and killed his soldiers in the river. He says they will be judged with fairness by the white man's laws. Iron Bow and the other chiefs must go to Fort Griffin to discuss a reservation for the Antelope."

Despite the distasteful proposals, Iron Bow was pleased with the proposition, not because he wanted to surrender the offenders and go to a reservation but because the captain considered Iron Bow the leader of a war party and thought it was concealed somewhere behind the rocks. "Iron Bow will discuss the long-knife captain's demands with his people. Let us meet here again at sundown."

After Yellow Dog's interpretation Captain Thomas became agitated and demanded a reply in one hour. Iron Bow slowly explained, "That decision is difficult. All the chiefs and the old men must be given opportunity to speak, and the speeches must be carefully weighed." Yellow Dog interpreted.

Captain Thomas drew a gold watch from his pocket. "It's nearly three o'clock. Tell the chief if we don't hear from him in one hour, we will attack. I'll fire a shot when half the time is up."

When Yellow Dog repeated this ultimatum, Iron Bow looked greatly disturbed. If the long-knife soldier attacked soon and killed him at once, they could, by riding hard, catch the band before nightfall. He needed to delay them most of the afternoon. In that time his people would be too far away to catch before dark; and by continuing their retreat through the night, they would be nearing Apache country. The long knife would not want to risk a conflict with both the Comanche and the Apache.

He said, "Tell the long knife what he wants takes time. Yellow Dog has seen a council meeting; he knows they cannot be done quickly. The Antelope will fight rather than take hasty actions to be regretted later. Tell him if there is a fight, many soldiers will die. Our number is greater than his. With a call, Iron Bow can bring two hundred warriors. But if a decision to give up the warriors could be reached after careful discussion, no one will die."

When he heard Iron Bow's reply, Captain Thomas looked unhappy and indecisive. He and the other soldier rode back toward the river for a conference. The one called Sergeant Quinn shook his head during most of the conversation. He was a short middle-aged man with a red nose and a big belly. After a few minutes the leader returned. "I know you wouldn't bring more than a hundred warriors, and they would be, no doubt, poorly equipped for war. Nevertheless, to avoid loss of more lives, yours and ours, I'll give you two hours and no more."

Yellow Dog concluded the message by pointing to where the sun would be in two hours; then he looked carefully at the rocks. Iron Bow shook his head. From his uncle, Juan Horse, he had long ago learned about the long-knife's times and measures. Two hours was not enough.

When Iron Bow attempted a reply, the long knife spun his horse around and trotted back into the river. Iron Bow returned to his hiding place and considered his predicament. The scouts, especially Yellow Dog, would be suspicious about the probability of a council meeting. Iron Bow had not brought any warriors with him to talk with the long knife, and they had seen or thought they had seen, only a few warriors during the ambush.

As he considered his situation, he tried to think what he would do if he were a long-knife chief. He would have to make preparations for an attack in case the Antelope would not give in to his demands. He would spend this time improving his position. Perhaps he would try to work around to the Antelope's back.

In his mind he reviewed the river five miles each side of his position. He remembered a rocky crossing near a twisted cottonwood three miles downriver. Though it was unsatisfactory for wagons, it was adequate for soldiers on good horses. He wished he could send out scouts.

Since the soldiers were well-concealed, Iron Bow would have to let his ears tell him what to do. As he lay quietly, the river brought him all the sounds of the long-knife. At first they were noisy; then they were quiet. He guessed they were taking naps in the warm sun. The young could always sleep anywhere and at any time.

He yearned to be young again, sitting straight on his horse, searching for the great buffalo herds. As he reflected on the halcyon days of his youth, he remembered the beauty and tenderness of his wives, Sunny Sky and Hears the Sun Rise. He was especially grateful to Hears the Sun Rise for giving him Jumping Bear, in whom he would live on here after leaving for the Great Spirit's hunting grounds.

What would that be like? How could it be better than what he had enjoyed here—before the white man? He was thankful to the Great Spirit that he could end his life still strong and full of courage, as had Fighting Eagle and his fathers before him.

Faintly, he heard horses well beyond the other side of the river. He waited. They were moving away. The long-knife chief thought he had been clever enough to have the soldiers lead their horses far enough from the river so the Antelope would not know he was going to cross downriver and come back.

He scrambled down to his horse and jumped on. He did not think he would have to worry about the noise of a single horse. Even if he did, he had no time. He must get to the downriver crossing before the soldier. He whipped the horse with his bow as they raced along the river.

Everything was more clearly defined and more beautiful than it had been during his whole life. The sky was bluer, the air was fresher and more invigorating, the birds sang more melodiously. And he was aware of renewed strength; each muscle felt resilient, ready to accomplish anything asked of it.

He urged his fine black horse, Shadow, to go faster. He had a long, smooth stride—the best horse he had ever ridden. He seemed to understand Iron Bow's pleasure as well as his sense of urgency. His hoofs barely touched the ground as they raced along with the slight wind to their backs.

Iron Bow reached the crossing before the soldiers, giving him time to select the best point for defense and attack. There was less vegetation than at the other place, but there were numerous hillocks and large rocks. Even though the situation was not favorable as the earlier one—he could not look down on the soldiers and pick his targets as carefully— he could move around more easily, changing his cover as he retreated. He hid his horse behind a hill and ran to an eight-foot boulder near the river, barely concealing himself before the soldiers arrived.

He heard splashing and shouting as they entered the water, and he could hear the chief's voice. He would have come along because he did not trust Yellow Dog. It was what Iron Bow would have done, himself.

With effort Iron Bow restrained himself. The scouts would be especially alert for the least movement along the bank. Once again, age and experience were on his side. As before, he waited until he felt sure the soldiers must be in the middle of the river and then waited a little longer. He placed an arrow in his bow. His first shot would have to be quick and accurate.

When he sprang into view, he was disappointed. Having drifted downriver, they were almost a hundred feet farther away than he had anticipated. He took quick aim at a soldier with a flag and ducked as bullets began to ricochet from the rocks around him. He heard a cry of pain and knew his arrow had found its target.

In his mind he reviewed what he had seen. The long-knife chief was just behind and to the right of the flag bearer. Iron Bow crawled closer and prepared to shoot again. Now the soldiers would be in easy range, or they would have turned around and headed toward the far shore and be out of range.

He jumped up from behind a pile of rocks that protected him from the knees down. The soldiers were less than three hundred feet away. He took careful aim and shot at Captain Thomas.

Iron Bow was exposed too long. One bullet tore flesh from the left side of his neck, and another hit his left leg. He slumped down and tested the leg. It was not bad. The bullet had gone through the fleshy part of his thigh, missing the bone. The neck wound was superficial. He would waste no time worrying about these wounds; the soldiers would be coming as fast as they could. Maybe he would have time for one more good shot. This time he would get the chief. He crawled to another spot.

A bullet glanced off his hipbone as he stood up, and another tore across his stomach just above his breech cloth. Unwaveringly, he picked out Captain Thomas, pleased to see the broken shaft of his earlier arrow protruding from the long knife's left hip. Iron Bow let fly again and ducked as another bullet furrowed his right temple. He staggered with dizziness for a moment but did not fall.

Bent low, he limped as fast as he could the sixty feet to the hill where he had hidden Shadow. Bullets kicked up dirt all around; one hit his right calf and made him hobble awkwardly the last few feet. Here again he felt the Great Spirit's favor; the bullet had missed the bone. He put a quieting hand on the black horse and then struggled to the top of the hill.

He was surprised to see the soldiers had dismounted and were taking cover. Two were helping the Captain, who had another arrow protruding from his body, this one in his chest. Death would be the price of his ignorance. A bullet tore across Iron Bow's left shoulder before he could pull his bow, and he sank behind a rock. He tested the shoulder anxiously—only a flesh wound. He could still hold the bow steady with it. He put his back to the rock and scanned the eastern horizon. There was dust about three miles away. Soon he would be surrounded if he did not move.

With great effort he pulled up onto his horse. They were running again. Despite the waves of weakness and the numerous wounds that covered his body with blood, he felt exhilaration. He was alive and riding. With the long-knife chief dead or nearly dead, the soldiers would have to take time to reorganize.

When he looked back, Iron Bow was excited to see a large number of soldiers in pursuit; only a few had stayed behind.

He had feared there would be few, if any, in pursuit. The chief must be dead, and his followers wanted revenge.

He had to keep them interested in the chase. One must never underestimate his enemy, even a poorly led one. The new leader would surely figure out before long that Iron Bow was diverting them from The People. If he did not figure it out, the scouts would tell him. Iron Bow decided on a course parallel to his people's, one on the opposite side of the Long-Ridge Mountains.

He looked over his shoulder after a long time of hard riding and saw the soldiers had fallen back at least a mile. He laughed aloud to see they had been joined by the second group. Nearly all the soldiers were chasing him, and he knew the mountains well. He could escape if that were his intention.

He kicked the sides of Shadow and called for a final surge of strength as the lathering animal labored to ascend the sloping south side of a big mesa the Antelope called The Sun's Table. It was a steep, rugged climb that few horses could make carrying a rider the size of Iron Bow.

Two bullets tore into Shadow's belly when they were within two hundred feet of the top. He jumped from the dead animal as it began sliding back down the mesa. With bleeding legs Iron Bow climbed the rest of the way. Bullets were again whizzing around him, and two more tore into his legs as he dragged himself onto the top and lay for a moment, gasping for breath. He took off his moccasins.

The sky was still blue, but the sun was sinking toward the horizon. Thousands of images of past battles and hunts flashed through his consciousness. And he saw the faces of his people, especially those of his sons and grandsons. He licked his cracked lips and took a drink from his water bag.

The water was tepid and tasted of leather, but it refreshed him. The feeling he had was like life itself. Life had been as refreshing as a drink of water when he really needed it. He wished it would last forever.

When he felt strong again, Iron Bow stood proudly, drawing his great bow. He saw a scout riding west toward the Antelope; it was Yellow Dog. He took careful aim, disregarding the bullets that hit or barely missed his body, and sent the arrow into Yellow Dog's back. He raised his bow defiantly over his head. "Come and get me, Long Knives," he shouted in their language. A bullet slammed into his chest and he fell back, resting his bloody head on a smooth rock.

Part 3:
COUNTING COUP

He sang quietly as he saw the red streaks in the western sky. Today he saved his people. Tomorrow he would ride with his fathers in the Great Spirit's hunting grounds. There The People are strong, the grass is always green, and the game is plentiful.

Babb, T. A. ("Dot"). *In the Bosom of the Comanches.* Dallas, 1912.

Catlin, George. *North American Portfolio.* London, 1844.

Canonge, Elliott. *Comanche Texts.* Norman, 1958.

Corwin, Hugh D. *Comanche and Kiowa Captives in Oklahoma and Texas.* Guthrie, Oklahoma, 1959.

Delaney, Robert. *The Southern Ute People.* Phoenix, 1974.

Dobie, J. Frank. *The Mustangs.* Boston, 1952.

Eastman, Edwin. *Seven and Nine Years among the Comanches and Apaches.* Jersey City, 1874.

Fehrenbach, R. T. *Comanches: The Destruction of a People.* New York, 1979.

Garretson, Martin. *The American Bison.* New York, 1938.

Gilles, Albert S. *Comanche Days.* Dallas, 1974.

Haley, James E. "The Comanchero Trade." *The Southwestern Historical Quarterly,* 38(January 1935) 157-76.

_____. "The Great Comanche War Trail." *The Panhandle-Plains Historical Review,* 23(1950) 1-11.

Handbook of North American Indians. ed. William C. Sturtevant. 15 vols. Wahington, D.C., 1978.

Harris, Caroline. *History of the Captivity and Providential Release Therefrom of Mrs. Caroline Harris.* New York, 1838.

Holt, Roy Davis. "Comanche Indian Horsemen." *The Cattleman.* September 1946, pp. 181-86.

Jefferson, James, Robert W. Delaney, and Gregory C. Thompson. *The Southern Utes: A Tribal History*. Ignacio, Colorado, 1972.

Lee, Nelson. *Three Years among the Comanches*. Albany, 1859.

Lehman, Herman. *Nine Years among the Indians (1870-79)*. Austin, 1927.

Newcomb, W. W., Jr. *The Indians of Texas*. Austin, 1961.

Plummer, Rachel. *Narrative of the Capture and Subsequent Sufferings of Mrs. Rachel Plummer during a Captivity of Tweny-one Months among the Comanche Indians; with a Sketch of Their Manners, Customs, Laws, &c, &*. 1839.

Rarey, John Soloman. *The Art of Taming Wild Horses*. London, 1874.

Richardson, Rupert. *The Comanche Barrier to South Plains Settlement. Glendale, 1933.

_____. *Along Texas Old Fort Trails*. Abilene, Texas, 1972.

Ruiz, Jose Francisco. *Report on the Indian Tribes of Texas in 1828*. New Haven, 1972.

Smith, Clinton L. and Jefferson D. *The Boy Captives*. Bandera, Texas, 1927.

Terrell, John Upton. *The Plains Apache*. New York, 1975.

Wallace, Ernest and E. Adamson Hoebel. *The Comanches: Lords of the Southern Plains*. Norman, 1952.

Wilson, Jane Adeline. *A Thrilling Narrative of the Sufferings of Mrs. Jane Adeline Wilson during Her Captivity among the Comanche Indians*. 1853.

Worcester, Donald E. *The Apaches: Eagles of the Southwest*. Norman, 1979.

Wright, Murial H. *A Guide to the Indians of Oklahoma*. Norman, 1951.